Allison, I'll find your body. I promise.

Melanie swiped the wetness from her cheeks and lowered herself into the grave. She picked up her trowel and searched for more bones.

An hour later, Melanie's headache had become unbearable, causing her stomach to roil. Her eyelids grew heavy. Something was off. She sat on the edge of the hole.

"Jason, help." Her words were slurred. She struggled to stay upright.

Jason knelt and came face-to-face with her. "What's wrong?"

"I don't know."

"Help me out here. What's the last thing you did?"

"I—I... Took a break a while ago. Only digging since."

His gaze flew to a spot behind her.

She wilted into him. Her vision tunneled, and darkness closed in.

"Keith! Grab the cooler and her bag!"

Jason's frantic voice registered, but her body had shut down.

His warm arms lifted her. Her head bobbed and landed on his shoulder.

His rhythmic breathing was the last thing she heard before the world went dark.

Two-time Genesis Award-winner **Sami A. Abrams** and her husband live in Northern California, but she'll always be a Kansas girl at heart. She enjoys visiting her two grown children and spoiling their sweet fur babies. Most evenings, if Sami's not watching sports, you'll find her engrossed in a romantic suspense novel. She thinks a crime plus a little romance is the recipe for a great story. Visit her at www.samiaabrams.com.

Books by Sami A. Abrams

Love Inspired Suspense

Buried Cold Case Secrets

BURIED COLD CASE SECRETS

SAMI A. ABRAMS

LOVE INSPIRED SUSPENSE
INSPIRATIONAL ROMANCE

LOVE INSPIRED® SUSPENSE
INSPIRATIONAL ROMANCE

ISBN-13: 978-1-335-55478-9

Recycling programs for this product may not exist in your area.

Buried Cold Case Secrets

This edition published by arrangement with Harlequin Books S.A.

For questions and comments about the quality of this book, please contact us at CustomerService@Harlequin.com.

Love Inspired
22 Adelaide St. West, 40th Floor
Toronto, Ontario M5H 4E3, Canada
www.LoveInspired.com

Printed in U.S.A.

Let all bitterness, and wrath, and anger, and clamour, and evil speaking, be put away from you, with all malice: And be ye kind one to another, tenderhearted, forgiving one another, even as God for Christ's sake hath forgiven you.
—*Ephesians* 4:31-32

This book is dedicated to my husband, Darren, and kids, Matthew and Melissa, who are always cheering me on. And to my law enforcement consultant, Detective James Williams, Sacramento Internet Crimes Against Children, who answers all my wild questions. You guys are the best!

ONE

Melanie Hutton's feet struck the dirt trail in a comfortable rhythm. The cool air filled her lungs and relieved the tension building inside her. She'd taken up jogging years ago to help process her pain and calm her panic attacks. The semidaily routine had saved her sanity in the months following her escape from captivity and the disappearance of her best friend Allison's body.

Grateful the mild winter weather allowed her to pound out her stress on the lake loop, she forced herself to take advantage of her peaceful surroundings before the first snow of the season decided to fall.

Evergreens and bare-limbed trees towered above. A mix of bushes and brambles lined the path, and the light streaming through the foliage warmed Melanie's skin. Her breathing followed the same pattern as her steps. In, in, out. In, in, out.

A week ago, she'd accepted a job here in Valley Springs, the town that once held fond memories of her childhood. Now, fifteen years later, the horrors of her and Allison's time shackled and beaten by a deranged man hovered like a raging storm. Her brain refused to release the details, but the terror continued to haunt her.

Pure determination had fueled her decision to return. She owed it to Allison to find her remains.

Melanie had intended to slip into town without announcement of her arrival. However, someone had taken it upon themselves to post news of her return on the local social media group for all to see. Looks of pity were not something she wanted. Nor were the glares of accusation. Within days of her escape, the town had taken sides. People either felt sorry for her, for what she'd endured, or they hated her for leaving Allison behind to die. As for her parents, they hadn't had her back. They'd been too worried about their reputation.

Why had she come home?

Slowing her run to a walk along the wooded trail, she placed her hands on her lower back and sucked in the crisp winter air. Memories of Allie during happier times flooded her mind. The two of them had come to the lake and explored the path often as teens. She missed her friend so much that her chest ached. Her phone buzzed, so she pulled it from her zippered pocket. She glanced at the screen. A text from Sheriff Monroe.

Know you aren't officially on the job yet. Hikers found some suspicious bones. Can you meet one of my detectives at Myers Trailhead?

Might as well. Melanie was already at the lake, so the jog back to the trailhead would only take ten minutes. Her thumbs flew over the keypad.

Heading there now.

Monroe responded within seconds.

Thanks. I owe you.

She smiled and tucked away her phone…along with the IOU, which she would claim at a later time.

Sparrows screeched and scattered, leaving an eerie silence. She scanned the adjacent brush.

What did the birds know that she didn't?

A cold shiver snaked down her spine. The bushes rustled, and tree limbs dangled like fingers reaching out to grab her. Her worst nightmare—the fear of captivity—threatened to grab hold and consume her.

"Calm down. Take a deep breath. Don't let the past control you." She spoke aloud, the words soft and deliberate. She'd overcome the worst of her post-traumatic stress from her abduction, but on occasion, panic rushed to the surface. This was one of those occasions. The necessity to escape clawed at her.

She spun to face the trail and took her first step.

A strong arm encircled Melanie's throat from behind and yanked her backward. Her attacker tightened his hold, cutting off her ability to scream.

Her fingers pulled at the sweatshirt-covered arm in a frantic attempt to get air.

The hulk of a man pulled her off the trail and into the woods. Her heartbeat pounded like a jackhammer, and black dots clouded her vision. If her assailant succeeded in getting her deeper into the brush, her life was over.

Think, Melanie. Think. Her mind cleared enough to formulate a plan. It was a long shot, but what choice did she have?

She inhaled and released her grip on his arm. Curving her fingers, she reached back and jammed her fingernails into his face, praying she struck his eyes.

His hold loosened as he howled in pain.

Melanie scrambled from his grasp. Her momentum sent her sprawling on the ground. Rocks and bark tore her hands and ripped through her black track pants, scraping her knees. Sucking in precious oxygen, she lifted her head and came eye-to-eye with a man in a ski mask. Hollow orbs stared back at her as he gripped her arm and leaned close.

The man's breath fanned her face, and his nails dug into her sleeves and pricked the skin on her arm.

Her heart thundered in her chest. She jerked away and gave her attacker a hard shove.

Surprised, he lost his balance and stumbled backward.

She staggered to an upright position and sprinted through the dense woods.

Tree limbs slapped against her. Her breath whooshed with each frantic step. She lost her balance and grasped a nearby tree. The bark sliced her skin, adding to the sting of her already damaged flesh. Tears pricked her eyes. The thought of being abducted again made her gut twist.

The sound of crunching footsteps tormented her as her assailant drew closer.

She prayed she'd chosen the right direction and that the trailhead and her car were not far.

Maybe staying off the path hadn't been a great idea, but the man-made trail put her out in the open. She had to get away and find help.

Make a plan and do it. Don't second-guess yourself.

Her pace quickened, and she stumbled on the uneven terrain. Her foot landed in a hole. Her ankle rolled. Landing with a thud, breath whooshed from her lungs. Pushing herself upright, she sprang to her feet and bit back a scream. Fire shot up her leg, but she surged on. She refused to die in the middle of nowhere.

Her gaze darted around the woods. *There.* Up ahead, a bramble of bushes. Melanie cringed at the thought of tiny thorns stabbing her, but she had limited choices.

Thankful for the protection of her long sleeves and pants, she skirted the edge of the thick blackberry vines and tucked in behind the tangled shrub. The sharp points tore into her skin.

Blood trickled down her arms and legs beneath her clothes. Her face stung from the scrapes she'd endured. But she was alive. So far, anyway.

Silence surrounded her. She strained to listen for a clue to her attacker's location.

Minutes dragged by. Nothing.

She exhaled and slipped from the prickly vines, receiving more cuts for her efforts. Her ankle throbbed, but she ignored it and took off in the direction of the parking lot. She hoped.

The sight of the trail ten feet away made her want to weep for joy. Relief flooded her as her location registered. Fifty yards from her car. She was going to make it. Hitting the path, she turned left and ran smack into pure muscle.

Arms closed around her.

She screamed and struggled against the powerful grip.

"Whoa. Take it easy," a deep baritone voice soothed.

She glanced up and gazed into the most vivid green eyes she'd ever seen.

He released her and stepped back, giving her space. "I'm with the Sheriff's department. You're safe with me."

The man's flannel shirt and jeans had her mind scrambling to put the pieces together.

Reality hit her like a two-by-four to the stomach and knocked the wind out of her.

He wasn't her attacker. He was worse.

Her best friend's brother, Jason Cooper, stood before her. The man who hated her guts.

* * *

The blood drained from the woman's face. She stared at him as if he'd introduced himself as a serial killer. Her facial features had a familiarity about them.

The air left Jason's lungs.

Melanie Hutton, his sister Allison's best friend. The friend who'd left Allie in the hands of a maniac to save her own hide. The desire to walk away flooded him, but Melanie appeared to be in trouble, and duty called him to help.

He fought the urge to cross his arms over his chest. "What happened?"

"Someone attacked me." Her teeth chattered.

"Explain."

Words flew from her mouth as she gave an account of being attacked on the trail, then chased through the woods and finally, running in to him. Literally.

Jason unsnapped his holster strap and hovered his hand over the Glock at his side. He scanned Melanie from head to toe. The scrapes and cuts covering her face and body made his heart rate kick up a notch.

"How about we get you back to my truck and take a look at those injuries?" His gaze darted along the edge of the trail. He may not like her, but no one deserved to be hunted like an animal.

"Thank you." She took a step and stumbled.

He steadied her. "You never mentioned you hurt your leg."

"I twisted my ankle when I escaped. I guess it stiffened when I stopped running." She straightened and pulled away.

"Listen." He pursed his lips. "I'll be honest. You're not my favorite person, but you need someone to lean on right now. Let me help you."

Her mouth fell open. "You want to help me?"

Did he? He sighed. His instincts told him Melanie's life was in danger, and he had to man up and protect her. "I'm not a monster."

"Never said you were," she mumbled.

He wrapped an arm around her waist and waited for her to lean against him.

She stiffened, but then, after a long exhale, she allowed him to take her weight.

As they ambled down the trail toward his vehicle, he scanned the area. He slid his hand into his pocket and clicked the unlock button on the truck remote. Supporting Melanie, he reached across and opened the passenger door.

"Let's sit you down and take a look at your wounds." He lifted her and eased her onto the seat.

She collapsed, leaning against the headrest.

Now, in a public area and off the wooded trail, he took inventory of her injuries. She would've looked better if she'd gone ten rounds with a grizzly bear.

"Hang on." He reached behind the seat and retrieved his first-aid bag. Placing it on the ground, he squatted and rummaged through it.

"That's quite the medical kit."

Jason met her gaze.

Had her eyes always been that brown and vulnerable? *Get it together, dude. She left your sister to die.*

He shook off the thought and pulled out a handful of antiseptic wipes.

"This is gonna sting." He dabbed the wet cloths on her scrapes and cuts.

She hissed in a breath. Tears trickled down her cheeks.

"I'm sorry." His grandma had taught him to cherish women and never hurt them. He hated causing her more pain.

"It has to be done." She bit her lower lip.

Several minutes later, he finished cleaning her wounds and applied cream to the abrasions.

"Time to take a look at that ankle." He bent and untied her tennis shoe.

"Jason!" Fear strangled her word.

His hand flew to his sidearm. He popped up and spun toward the direction of Melanie's stare. A shadowed figure ducked into the brush along the edge of the parking lot and out of sight.

So much for safety in a public place. Jason snatched the cell phone from his belt holder and dialed his partner's number.

"Hey, Keith. I need backup at Myers Trailhead. West entrance."

"On it," Keith replied.

Jason had come to Myers Lake Park, following the report of a suspicious find by a group walking the trail. According to the call, hikers had discovered bones near the lake, and he'd drawn the short straw to come investigate.

Jason placed himself between her and the suspect. His instincts told him to pursue the man, but his training said to keep the victim safe. He'd stay by her side, for now.

After one last survey of the area, he turned his attention back to Melanie. He kneeled and wrapped an ice pack on her ankle. "My partner will be here in a few. I need to go check out a possible crime scene. I'll have him escort you to the hospital."

"Not a chance."

He blinked. "Excuse me?" Standing, he leveled his gaze on her.

"I said no." She brushed the hair from her face. "I'm going with you."

Of all the ridiculous ideas. Jason fisted his hands on his hips. "You need to see a doctor."

She slid from the truck and wobbled. He grabbed her arm and stabilized her. "I have a job to do. Maybe you haven't heard, but I'm the forensic anthropologist your department hired. Besides, the sheriff already asked me to accompany you."

He clenched his jaw. Yeah, he'd heard she'd taken the job, but he'd convinced himself she'd never return to Valley Springs. The Lord had to be playing a joke on him. Putting him and Melanie together in the same room was like throwing gas on a fire. But to work together?

"Look, if you have a problem with it, talk to your boss," she challenged.

Keith pulled into the parking lot, saving Jason from having to respond.

How would he survive working with the person who sentenced his sister to death?

Grateful for the walking stick Jason had begrudgingly found her, Melanie hobbled along the trail.

Keith hadn't verbally questioned her presence, but she'd seen the look he'd aimed at Jason. Trusting his partner, Keith had positioned himself on one side of her and Jason on the other. The trio walked along in silence, Jason carrying an evidence-recovery kit and Keith a camera.

Happy for the moment of quiet, she took the opportunity to calm her mind. She inhaled the crisp winter air and focused on the beauty of her surroundings. After escaping the brutality of her captor as a teen, she'd experienced horrible flashbacks and panic attacks for years. Over time, she'd harnessed control of her extreme reactions, but she'd never released the guilt of leaving her friend behind.

Maybe she should tell Jason about her PTSD, but that was her own business. Besides, the man hated her. She didn't want his pity, as well. Her shoulders slumped as she continued the trek.

The sun flashed through the trees, highlighting the spot of her attack. A shiver snaked down her spine. She trudged on to the location of her first assignment.

Three hikers stood on the edge of the trail, huddled together.

"Afternoon, folks." Jason introduced himself, took their personal information and listened while the group explained what they'd come across. "And where did you find these bones?"

"There." The woman pointed at the small opening in the thick bushes.

Melanie ducked under the dangling tree limbs and pushed past the brush, adding to her scrapes and cuts.

Jason passed the bag to Keith and approached the disturbed soil with caution. He sat on his haunches and studied the bones protruding from the earth, then turned to the hikers. "How in the world did you see that from the trail?"

"We didn't." One of the guys piped up. "Sharon had to, um, go. So she ducked behind the bushes. That's when we heard her scream and found those." The man pointed to the three to four inches of brownish-colored bones peeking from the packed Indiana soil.

"Thanks for calling it in. We'll be in touch if we need additional information."

"Sure thing." The group strolled on but continued to look over their shoulders until they were out of sight.

Jason pivoted on the balls of his feet and reached into

his jacket. He pulled out blue nitrile gloves and snapped them on. "Keith, hand me an evidence bag, would you?"

"Wait." She held her hand out to Jason's partner. "We need to take pictures first."

The man shifted his gaze to Jason, as if asking permission.

Jason shrugged. "Why not. Partner, I'd like to introduce you to the new forensic anthropologist you've been hearing about. And, if I'm not mistaken, our newly appointed coroner."

She nodded. Most forensic anthropologists carried two jobs. Usually, the second was in a lab or as a professor. How she'd landed the appointment as Forensic Anthropologist and part-time Anderson County coroner was beyond her. She hadn't even applied for the position. Sheriff Monroe had offered, and she'd accepted.

Keith raised an eyebrow. "Okay, then." He handed her the camera. "Welcome to the team."

Jason grunted—the fact that he still blamed her after all these years was obvious.

Well, he could hold a grudge all he wanted. No one hated her more than she hated herself for leaving Allison behind.

Turning her focus to the job at hand, she grasped the camera and grimaced. Her palms burned from the cuts. She slipped the strap around her neck and snapped pictures of the scene from multiple angles, then zeroed in on the bones.

Satisfied she had sufficient documentation, she nodded at Jason. "I think I got enough photos."

He rolled his eyes. "Look, we don't even know if this is a crime scene yet. Those bones could be from an animal for all we know."

"Then let's find out." Melanie brushed past him and

kneeled on the ground next to the dingy white objects. A whimper escaped her lips. Her body protested every move. She gazed up at Jason and extended her hand. "Gloves, please."

He slapped the items into her hand and crossed his arms.

It only took a few seconds to verify her suspicions. "Nope, not animal. These look human. See the three distal and middle phalanges? If these bones extend beneath the surface, there's enough evidence to work an exhumation." She swung her hand in a horizontal arc. "A body shouldn't be buried out here."

Keith dug in the kit and produced an evidence marker. He placed it next to the bones and snapped a picture. "She's right, man."

The glare Jason pointed at his partner had her biting her lip to keep from smiling. The last thing Jason Cooper wanted to admit was that she was right.

Melanie dusted the soil from the bones, careful to keep the sediments in a pile close to the evidence. Her movements went on autopilot.

Two inches below the surface, she had no doubt the bones were human. Four inches later, she had her confirmation. A body—or at least a partial one—laid beneath the surface.

She stood and bit back a moan. The aches and pains had intensified. "Well, boys. It's time to tape off the area. Give me a ten-foot radius out from this open clearing."

"Excuse me?" Jason stepped closer and peered at her crude work. "Is that—?"

"Yes. That's a hand." She pointed to another bone. "And there's the tip of the radius and ulna. In my professional opinion, we have a grave site or, at minimum, a hand and arm that requires identification."

Jason's mouth twisted. He huffed, then called over his shoulder, "Keith, let's cordon this off and call the sheriff."

The men began securing her find, leaving her alone with her thoughts.

Why would someone bury a body out here in the middle of nowhere?

Her pulse rate skyrocketed. She'd hyperfocused on the scene and had forgotten about the man who'd attacked her. Her gaze darted along the perimeter of the small clearing. She jerked at the shiver across her shoulder blades. Had the assailant tried to kill her or scare her? If he intended to kill, why? Her gaze drifted to the grave.

The bones called to her.

Gingerly squatting next to them, she tilted her head and mulled over the events and the evidence in front of her.

She glanced around and realized her attack hadn't been far from here. Had the man in the dark hoodie come after her specifically, or had the visitation to his victim's final resting place been interrupted? Either option made her stomach roil.

One thing she knew for sure, she had a job to do, and working with a hostile Jason wouldn't be easy.

"Just talked with the boss man." Jason pivoted to face Melanie and slid his phone into his pocket. "He wants you to stop at the hospital for treatment, then go home and get a good night's sleep."

Melanie shook her head. "I need to get started. My supplies are in my SUV. If you'll help me carry them down here—"

"No go, Mel." Jason sucked in a breath. He hadn't called her by her nickname since the time of her and Allison's kidnapping. The familiar moniker flooded his mind with memories of the two innocent girls he used to tease. He swallowed past the lump in his throat. "Sheriff wants you checked out. Keith will stay until a deputy arrives to stand watch over the scene."

"I don't need a doctor." She straightened her spine in challenge and limped toward him.

He cocked an eyebrow. "Really? That's why you can barely walk?"

The pain and fatigue etched on her face made him want to retract his words. He might hold her responsible for Allison's disappearance, and presumed death, but he had a heart somewhere beneath all the anger. Didn't he?

Her chin dropped to her chest, and she refused to look at him. "Okay."

He rubbed the back of his neck. "Ah, man, I know you've had a rough day. I shouldn't have— Well, let's just say I'm sorry."

Tears spilled, and she swiped them away. "No, the sheriff's right. If I jump in now, I'll be sloppy and miss something." She turned and wobbled away, leaning heavily on the walking stick.

The woman had brought nothing but pain and grief to the forefront of his life again. So why did he feel ashamed of himself for treating her like dirt?

He jogged to catch up. "I'll take you to the hospital."

She jerked to a halt and rounded on him. "You're telling me what to do?"

His jaw clenched. "I don't think…" No, he wouldn't go there.

Her eyes lit with fire. "Go ahead. Say it," she dared him.

She had baited him, and he knew it, but his mouth had a mind of its own. "I don't think you make the best choices. At least you didn't with my sister."

"And you have no idea what you're talking about. Have you ever listened to me? Have you ever looked at the evidence without prejudice?" She spun and hobbled down the trail.

He hadn't needed to listen to Melanie's story. She'd left his sister in the hands of a killer. Period. He'd studied the case more times than he could count over the last fifteen years. It's why he'd volunteered to help investigate cold cases when the leads had dried up. He knew what had happened. The fault of losing his sister landed on Melanie.

The woman had induced a tension headache. He massaged his temples and wondered what he had done wrong for God to hate him so much.

Birds chirped in the trees and the bushes rustled with wildlife. The peaceful sounds eased Jason's nerves.

But what if it wasn't animals?

His senses surged on high alert. He might hold a grudge against Melanie, but he refused to allow her to get hurt on his watch. Quickening his pace, he fell in step a few feet behind her and unsnapped his holster strap again.

Hand hovering over his duty weapon, he scanned his surroundings, determined to protect the one person he had hoped never to see again.

TWO

Who was in charge of the temperature in the emergency room? Melanie shivered beneath the thin cotton gown. Of course, the open back didn't help.

The antiseptic odor assaulted her nose and caused bile to rise in her throat. She hated hospitals. They reminded her of the past. She'd spent an entire week recovering from her injuries in this same building, jumping at every sound. And the hospital had no shortage of sounds.

White paper crinkled under her as she shifted on the hard mattress. Her ankle throbbed, and she peered at the scrapes that traced her limbs. Tears pricked. The attack played like a film reel in her head.

The thick arm across her throat. The hot, rancid breath on her face. Fingers digging into her skin. And those eyes. She knew those eyes, but from where? Her present or her past?

Tears trickled over her cheeks and dripped off her chin. If only she could remember, then Jason could lock the guy up, and she'd be free to continue with her self-imposed mission.

Twenty-four hours ago, she'd arrived in Valley Springs. Returning to her childhood hometown had the same effect as a kick to the teeth. But a new job awaited her with the Anderson County Sheriff's Department, and maybe she'd reach her goal and solve the mystery of the location of Allison's body. Anyone in their right mind knew her friend had died. The amount of blood discovered in the cabin pointed to that conclusion. Her job—not the one the sheriff's department or county hired her to do, but her personal duty—was to bring closure to herself, Jason and the town. Her amnesia from the traumatic experience had protected her mentally but had also repressed the details of what had happened, along with the identity of her abductor. If not for her guilty conscience of leaving Allison behind, and the man who'd killed her still walking free, she'd never have set foot in Valley Springs again.

Salty liquid stung the cuts on her palm when she swiped at the wetness. "Why, God?" A sob escaped her lips.

"Mel?"

Her gaze rose to the curtain separating the area from other patients.

Jason held the white cloth aside and peered in. "What's wrong?"

He had to be kidding, right? She might as well be honest with the man. It wasn't as if he didn't have the ability to look at her and come to his own conclusion. "You mean besides feeling as though I've been dragged behind a truck on gravel?"

"Sorry. Bad question on my part. Sheriff's here. We need to interview you, if you're ready."

She raised an eyebrow. *Sure, let me entertain people in my lovely ball gown.* "I guess so." Leaning forward, she grabbed the extra blanket draped at the foot of the bed. Teeth gritted, she lifted the cover, reclined and drew the bedspread to her chin.

Jason pulled back the curtain, and Sheriff Dennis

Monroe waltzed in and stood next to her. Dennis, the man who'd asked her out when they were teenagers more times than she cared to admit, stood before her, hat in his hands. She'd never accepted his invitations. He'd been four years her senior, and it hadn't felt right. Although, to be honest, age had nothing to do with it. She'd only had interest in one young man. Her best friend's brother.

"Dennis."

"Melanie. It's good to see you again. Thanks for checking out the report of the bones." He fiddled with the brim of his hat. "What'd the doctor say?"

"Said I'd be sore and to take it easy, but we know I can't do that. Those bones have to be exhumed before the ground hardens. We're fortunate we've had a mild season so far."

"Glad to hear it. Do you feel like giving Detective Cooper your statement about the attack? I'd like to listen if that's okay." Before she answered, the sheriff scooted a chair close to her bed and sat. He crossed one booted foot over the opposite knee.

"Sure. Might as well get it over with." Her gaze met Jason's.

He stood behind his boss, raised his brow and shrugged. "Whenever you're ready." He pulled a notepad from his pocket and waited for her to begin.

She rubbed the base of one palm with her opposite thumb, careful not to touch the road rash she'd acquired. "I arrived at my apartment yesterday and decided to go for a jog early this afternoon."

Jason cocked his head to one side. "Since when did you take up jogging? The Mel I knew hated to run."

"My therapist recommended it for my anxiety. I've learned to love it." She pulled at a loose thread on her blanket. "Anyway, when I stopped for a second to take in the scenery, a man came from behind and dragged me into the woods."

"Did you get a good look at him?"

Dennis dropped his foot to the floor and leaned forward.

Jason studied him for a moment and returned his attention to her.

"No. At first he had a choke hold on me from behind, then when I did get a look at him, he had on one of those face masks you wear in cold weather. You know, the kind with holes for the eyes and mouth." She placed her hand over her nose and chin, demonstrating the piece of cloth. "But, I saw his eyes." She shivered. Why couldn't she remember where she'd seen them before?

"Melanie?" Jason's low timbre pulled her from her jumbled thoughts.

"They seemed familiar, but I can't figure out why."

The sheriff rested against the back of his chair, seeming a little more relaxed. "No idea?"

"Not a clue." She sucked in a breath and winced. "I scrambled to get away and ran. That's when I collided with Jason."

Staring at the cream-colored wall, she thought through her day. A chill settled over her.

"What is it?" Jason stepped closer.

"I'm not sure. But I think someone's been watching me."

"Since when?"

"Since this morning, but I don't have any proof. Just a feeling."

"Who'd you make mad now?" Jason growled. His accusation hit her square the chest.

She glared at him, challenging him to say more.

Dennis jumped in before Jason could continue his

jabs. "Any enemies from your previous job? Someone you helped put behind bars?"

Her attention returned to the sheriff. "No enemies. Most of the cases I've worked have been recoveries after the person has gone to jail. Or the identification of missing persons."

Mouth twisted to the side, Dennis scratched his jaw. "That leaves ex-boyfriends. Any we need to consider?"

"No." As if. Melanie had kept her focus on her career. Pain from a relationship was the last thing she wanted. She'd had too much of that in her life already.

"All right then. If you don't mind, I'd like to have Keith check with your previous employer, University of North Texas, and with the Texas Rangers. See if they know something you don't."

"Whatever you feel is necessary." She rubbed her temples. "But I don't think you'll find anything."

"What about your move back? Who knows you're in town?" Jason held his pen poised to write.

"Other than everyone?" Okay, maybe she should tone down her bratty attitude. But the adrenaline had faded, and her nerves sparked. She pulled in air through her nose. "After checking my email this morning, I decided to take a look at the local social media group. I wanted to see what the scuttlebutt was around town. I noticed that someone announced my arrival on the local page this morning."

Dennis fiddled with his bootlace. "That had to be Gayle. She's our town crier around here."

"And all-around busybody," Jason muttered. "I guess that's it for now, unless you can think of anything else."

She shook her head. She hadn't a clue as to why the man attacked her.

Dennis slapped his thighs. "Well, I'll let Jason take care of springing you from this joint, and I'll contact

Keith." He rose and extended his hand. Glancing at her torn palms, he retracted his handshake. "I hope to see you in the office soon. I'm looking forward to working with you." With that, the man exited at a quick clip.

Jason's gaze followed his boss through the opening in the curtain.

"Jason?"

He spun.

"Everything okay?" She tilted her head and considered him. He'd filled out over the years. No longer the teenage boy she'd known. His face had a few more lines, but the same Jason still resided beneath the surface. And, unfortunately for her, his anger hadn't faded.

He shook his head. "Yeah, it's all good."

"Why don't I believe you?" Had he thought he could fool her? She'd known him too long for that.

"Look, sorry about that jerk question earlier. Let's get you discharged and safely tucked into your parents' old house since it has a security system."

"I'm not going there. I have an apartment near downtown. A place just off the square."

"All right, your place then." He looked confused but didn't say anything.

The thought of being alone in her apartment made her heart race. But what other choice did she have? She'd left town and had never returned, until now. She'd lost track of friends, and if she was honest, she didn't want to see them. The guilt and shame of the past continued to plague her.

"Sounds good to me." Not really, but admitting that to him was out of the question.

Jason took a few steps and paused. He scratched the stubble on his jaw. "Why don't you want to stay at your

parents' old place? They use it as a rental property, and
I know it's empty right now. It would be safer."

Her stomach flipped and threatened to erupt. Her parents had turned their backs on her when she'd fallen
apart in the hospital after the worst experience of her
life. When her mom had accused her of horrible things
after her abduction, and her dad hadn't defended her,
she'd grabbed her belongings and left town. Two days
later, she moved in with her aunt Heather in Texas. Too
bad the sweet woman had died years ago. Melanie sure
could use her aunt's advice right now.

"Not happening. I haven't been back there since I left
fifteen years ago. Aunt Heather told me they'd moved to
Florida. I didn't even know they'd kept the place."

His forehead crinkled. "Why?"

"Let's just say I have no desire to ask my parents for
anything."

He opened his mouth then shut it. "I'll get the doc."
Jason strode out of her little room.

Tears burned. But she refused to let them fall.

Stuck in a town that pitied her, working with a man
who hated her, and in pain because someone tried to hurt
her—what a mess. Why had God brought her back here?
No matter the reason, she trusted Him, but it didn't mean
that it wasn't hard.

Dr. Jenson entered. A smile adorned his face. "I hear
you want to fly the coop."

"Yes, sir." The sooner, the better. Even if a lonely
apartment awaited Melanie. She glanced at Jason, who
stood with arms crossed over his chest like a sentinel.
His protective stance puzzled her. For someone who held
a grudge, he sure had taken it upon himself to watch out
for her.

"I don't see why not. Just take it easy for a few days."

The man plunged his hand into his white lab coat and pulled out a pen. He scribbled his signature on a couple of pages fastened to a clipboard. "I'll let the nurses know. Someone will be in soon to help you with your belongings and your discharge instructions."

She pulled her attention back to the older man. "Thanks."

"No problem." He waved her off and hurried from the room, lab coat flapping in his wake.

After the nurse helped her dress and gave her the final release orders, she sat in a wheelchair and waited for Jason to pull his truck to the curved drive at the entrance of the hospital.

The cool breeze sent wisps of hair fluttering across her face. She tucked the errant strands behind her ear. A shiver rippled up her spine, and it had nothing to do with the temperature. Someone was watching her.

She scanned the edge of the parking lot. No movement.

"Ready?"

She jolted.

"Sorry. Didn't mean to startle you." Jason squinted, studying her. "Everything okay?"

"Fine." Melanie took Jason's offered hand and carefully rose from the wheelchair. Her body protested. "I feel like I'm a hundred and four."

He opened the passenger door and assisted her inside.

"Thanks." Gingerly grabbing the seat belt, she pulled it across herself and snapped the buckle.

"Don't mention it." Jason closed her door, jogged around the front of the truck and hefted himself in the driver's seat. "Address?"

The man was all business. If that's the way he wanted it, so be it. She'd come back to Valley Springs to find closure. To find her friend's body and regain her memory of the missing events surrounding her and Allison's captivity. Not to convince Jason he was wrong about her. How could she, when uncertainty of her role in her best friend's disappearance clouded her day-to-day life?

"One-oh-two Main Street."

He made his way through town, parked in front of her apartment and hurried to help her out of the vehicle.

Her second story apartment, located above a store that had gone out of business several years ago, sat at the edge of downtown. Jason held her elbow and escorted her up the exterior stairs.

A minute later, she opened the front door of her new home and stepped to the side.

Jason brushed past her and perused the small living area, where her boxes sat along the wall. "I see you haven't fully moved in."

"Like I said, I arrived yesterday. Haven't had much of a chance." She yawned. "Sorry. I guess today is catching up with me."

"No worries. I'll leave you to get some rest." He pulled out a business card and jotted something on the back. Holding the card between his index and middle finger, he extended it to her. "Here's my cell number. Call me when you're ready to head to the grave site."

Not pleased she'd have an escort tomorrow, she let out a long stream of air and took the card from him. "Plan for first thing in the morning."

He arched an eyebrow.

"Look. I need to finish before the weather changes and the ground freezes. I'm sorry you're stuck picking me up. I'll grab my SUV tomorrow, and then you'll be off the hook."

"Melanie. Yes, I'm still angry, but I have a job to do, and so do you." He opened his mouth, then closed it and sighed. "I asked Keith to move your SUV to the station, so don't worry about that. I'll be back at seven to pick you up."

"I appreciate it." She moved to the entrance and held open the door. "See ya later."

She closed the door behind Jason and slumped onto the couch. How had her life become such a disaster? *God, I wish I knew what You were up to.*

Her energy waned, and her lids drooped shut...

A hand covered her mouth, and a man whispered in her ear. What had he said? Her heart threatened to beat out of her chest. She had to escape.

She bolted from the couch. Panting, her gaze darted around the room. She gulped in air. The same nightmare had plagued her for years. She brushed the sweat from her brow, then ambled over to the window and peered into the night.

The streetlights glowed, and a single car passed along the otherwise deserted street. She'd missed her childhood town. All the fond memories of going for ice cream after baseball games and listening to live concerts at the town square tugged at her heart.

Her gaze hovered at the tree line across the road. She squinted. A figure stood in the shadows, his or her attention on Melanie's apartment.

A squeak passed her lips, and she slammed her bruised body against the wall next to the window.

Jason's phone number. Where had she put it? She crawled to the end table. Card in hand, she fumbled for her phone. Her trembling fingers refused to cooperate.

Whoever had Melanie in his or her sights had found her.

"Hey, Dad." Jason rested back against his recliner. He'd dropped off Melanie and had come straight home.

His temples throbbed. The day had sucked the energy from him. When he'd gotten the report of the bones along the trail, of all the things he'd thought he might find, Melanie had never come to mind.

"What's up, son?" The voice of his father, Ben, echoed through the phone.

"Thought I'd better call and tell you the latest news before you heard it from someone else." He rubbed his forehead. "Melanie's officially back in town."

Silence met his statement.

"Dad?"

"Yeah, I heard you. Saw it on the town's social media group. Does she remember anything?"

"Not that I know of, but I haven't asked." He had no intention of listening to the woman when it came to his sister's case. She'd lost his trust a long time ago.

"Why on earth not?" his dad growled.

"Because I don't want to hear what she has to say."

"You need to find out," Ben demanded.

"Then you talk to her." If his father wanted the information so badly, he could get it himself.

"Don't bring that woman anywhere near me."

Jason straightened in his seat. He understood anger, but his dad's tone bothered him.

A crunching sound and the whistle of the wind crossed the phone line. "Dad? Where are you?

"Just stepped outside, that's all." His father's voice was barely above a whisper.

What was his dad up to now?

Jason received a call every few days from the local bar and had to leave work to go pick up his drunken father. Throughout his childhood, Ben Cooper had been supportive and loving. But after Allison's disappearance, the man started visiting the bar, and the frequency of his trips had increased every year since.

His phone beeped, signaling another caller. His father would have to wait. "Listen, Dad, I have to go. I'll call you later."

He switched over. "Cooper."

"Help." A strangled female voice met his ear.

"Melanie?" He straightened in his seat.

"Jason, someone's out there."

He bolted from his chair and grabbed his keys from the side table. "Where?"

"Across the street in the tree line," she whimpered. "Please, help me."

"Lock the door and stay away from the windows. I'm on my way." He sprinted to his truck and raced down the street. Turning left, he aimed his vehicle toward downtown. He lived five minutes from Melanie's new place, but it seemed like thirty. He whipped into a parking spot in front of her apartment, slammed the vehicle into Park and threw open the driver's-side door. He scanned the tree line. Finding nothing, he rushed to the entrance and took the stairs two at a time. His pulse whooshed in his ears as sweat beaded on his forehead.

Hand on his weapon, he slid it from the holster and held it beside his leg. He pounded on Melanie's front door. "Mel, it's me. Open up."

The door creaked open, and she peered through the small slit between the frame and the edge of the door. "Jason." She threw it open and flung herself into his arms.

"Come on. Let's get you inside." Jason shuffled them into her apartment and closed the door. "I'm here. You're okay now."

Melanie's body shook against him.

He gave her a minute to calm down, then holstered his weapon and led her to the sofa. "Have a seat and tell me what happened."

"I fell asleep on the couch, and when I woke up, I wanted to enjoy the town lights on the square. They're so beautiful." She sucked in a ragged breath. "Anyway, I was looking out the window when I saw someone standing in the shadows staring back at me."

"Are you sure the person was looking at you and not just out for a walk and stopped to take a break?"

"You think I've lost my mind?" She gaped at him. Her voice rose in volume. "I know what I saw."

"Calm down. I believe you." He stood and strode to the window. Peering across the road, the shadow of trees caught his attention. "So, was the person in the street or on the sidewalk?"

She sniffed. "He was hiding beneath the trees."

"Are you sure it was a man?"

"No, I'm not. I only saw a figure. But after today..." Her voice trailed off.

She probably saw an animal, but he couldn't deny the fear-filled expression on the woman's face. He pivoted and studied her a moment. "Will you be all right if I go take a look?"

Her wide eyes pierced his heart. For a split second, she reminded him of the young, innocent girl he'd once known. "I promise I'll be right outside. I won't leave you."

With shaky fingers, she brushed a strand of hair from her face and nodded.

Jason walked to the door and turned the knob. "Secure the door behind me." He stepped outside and waited to hear the lock slide into place.

Satisfied that Melanie was safe in her apartment, he strode to his truck. Jason zipped his coat and flipped the collar to warm the back of his neck. The temperature had dropped, threatening a freeze in the coming days. He glanced into the night sky. Soon, snow would cover the small town and turn it into an artist's dream. He inhaled the cold air and considered praying for the first time in what seemed like forever.

He pulled his duty flashlight from underneath the seat and flicked it on. An owl hooted amid the trees, and a few blocks over, a dog barked against the backdrop of night. Under normal circumstances, the sounds comforted him, but tonight, the hairs on his nape stood at attention. Shaking off his ill ease, he crossed the street. He fisted his light and scanned the foliage. The beam illuminated the dark places under the trees.

Sweeping the ground one final time, his light revealed a shoe print. He bent down and examined the impression and the surrounding area. Crushed leaves and twigs left him curious as to how long the imprint had existed. His gut said not long. In places, the edges of the foliage had started popping back to their original positions.

He pulled his cell phone from his pocket and dialed the sheriff. His high-school buddy Dennis Monroe had climbed the ranks of the sheriff's department at an outstanding speed. When the good people of Anderson County voted him in, no one had been surprised. Jason hadn't minded their boss/employee relationship. He'd never wanted to be more than a detective, and he'd reached that goal a few years ago. His friend could have the politics and paperwork. He was happy solving crimes and bringing justice to those who deserved it.

"Hey, Dennis. I'm at Melanie's. It appears someone was watching her from across the street. I don't have any equipment to take a shoe impression or photos. Besides, this is Valley Springs PD's jurisdiction. Since this isn't exactly a crime scene, can you call VSPD and request an officer to come over?"

"Will do. Is she okay?"

"A little shook up, but I'll go back in to check on her once patrol arrives. Let me give you her address."

"Already have it. I'll make sure an officer arrives shortly."

Of course, Dennis had Melanie's address. The man had hired her. Jason had to ask her on the way home from the hospital—a fact that irritated him. He and Melanie had once been close, and now he knew little about her. But that's the way he wanted it, right? "I'll be waiting."

He disconnected and glanced up at her window. A second-story apartment with no visibility inside from this angle. What had the person tried to do?

Movement at the glass had him taking another look.

Melanie peered down at him. She hunched her shoulders and pulled her sweater tighter around herself.

He waved and received the same gesture in return.

After today's events, he wondered if she'd sleep tonight. Not a great possibility. And now? He knew one thing for sure. He couldn't leave her alone. Mad at her or not, she'd been Allison's best friend. He owed it to his sister.

The patrol officer arrived, and Jason gave her instructions. He made his way back to Melanie's apartment, scanning the street as he went. Nothing seemed out of place except for the uncertainty in his gut.

The door flew open. "What did you find?"

"Have a seat and let's talk."

She ushered him to the kitchen table, handed him a mug and retrieved the carafe. "Don't worry. It's decaf." She forced a smile. "I needed something warm to drink and thought you might, too."

He shrugged out of his jacket and hung it over his chair. He rubbed his hands together as Melanie poured his drink.

After putting the coffee pot on a hot pad, she eased herself onto the seat kitty-corner to him.

Gripping the mug, he inhaled the bold aroma. "Thanks. It's getting a bit chilly out there."

"I'm surprised it hasn't hit below freezing yet. It's a strange winter, that's for sure."

He stared into the dark liquid. He'd known the day would come he'd see Melanie again. The awful words he'd planned to spew at her refused to fall from his lips. He'd never imagined danger surrounding their reunion. The anger inside him eased. At least for the moment. "It is weird for us not to have snow by now."

She quirked an eyebrow. "Well, look at us. Talking about the weather."

The entire situation had *awkward* stamped all over it. He shrugged. "How 'bout them Colts."

She rolled her eyes. "As if that's any better."

His attempt to cover a laugh failed, and she joined in.

"So what did you find?" She brought the cup to her lips.

His gaze toured the small apartment. No decorations and few boxes to unpack. Either the woman had claimed a minimalist lifestyle, or she hadn't collected much over the years.

Jason brought his attention back to Melanie and proceeded to explain his discovery. Once he'd given her the details, they discussed her attacker and what she'd seen across the street.

Thirty minutes later, he stood. "You gonna be okay?"

"Yeah, I'm good." She twirled a strand of hair. A habit she'd acquired at a young age.

He walked to the door and paused. "I'll pick you up at seven, and we'll hit the office."

"I was hoping to go straight to the burial site."

"If it's all the same to you, I'd rather we let the temps climb a little before standing outside all day."

"There is that. Okay then, the office it is. You can show me around the station."

"Sounds like a plan." He exited her apartment. After confirming the lock had clicked into place, he meandered down the stairs to his truck. What had just happened? He'd spent an entire half-hour with the woman he'd vowed never to forgive. True, their conversation revolved around her stalker, but old affectionate emotions had knocked on his heart. He clenched his jaw, refusing to give in to his sentimental nudging. "Remember, she abandoned your sister and left her to die," he muttered as he scanned the neighborhood one more time before sliding into the driver's seat.

Hand on the ignition, he couldn't bring himself to leave her. The expression of fear on Melanie's face was seared into his brain. He had to stay. No matter what she'd done in the past, they'd grown up together. Had been friends at one time.

Disgusted with himself for even considering leaving her alone and unprotected, he jumped out and grabbed his emergency sleeping bag from the back seat. Returning to the driver's seat, he turned the key and cranked on the heater. He warmed the truck on and off throughout the night but refused to drive away and leave her vulnerable to another attack.

He had to protect her. Didn't he?

THREE

Jason rolled his neck in an attempt to relieve the crick he'd managed to acquire overnight. He lowered himself from the truck and made his way to Melanie's front door, hoping the woman had coffee made.

He'd gotten a few hours of shut-eye, but between watching her entry and the cold temperatures, sleep hadn't come easily.

When he knocked, Melanie cracked open the door and peered out.

She glanced at her watch then let him in. "You're a few minutes early. Would you like some coffee?"

"I'd love some." He ran a hand through his mussed hair.

"You look awf— You look tired," she amended and narrowed her gaze. "Wait a minute. Did you sleep in your truck last night?"

So much for being sneaky. "What gave me away?"

"Oh, I don't know. Maybe the rumpled clothes and the messy hair." She bit her lip to hide a smile.

He glanced down at his attire. He hadn't considered his clothing. "Guilty as charged."

"Come on and have a seat. I'll bring you a mug of caffeine and a couple of biscuits and bacon." She waved him to the kitchen table.

"Sounds amazing." He plopped down on a chair.

"Why didn't you tell me you planned to stay?"

What should he say? That she looked frightened? That she reminded him of the little girl he once knew? Or that his sister would've killed him if he hadn't taken care of her best friend? No, he couldn't say any of those things. Melanie had arrived in Valley Springs two days ago, and her presence had flipped his world upside down.

"I wanted to make sure no one bothered you last night. I didn't think you'd accept my help, so I didn't say anything."

She spun and gaped at him.

He quirked an eyebrow. "What?"

"I just thought… Never mind. Thank you for sacrificing your night." She placed a mug in front of him.

It hadn't been that big of a deal, had it? Maybe it had, but not protecting her hadn't sat well with him.

Melanie placed plates full of breakfast on the table. "Dig in. Then you can go wash up in the bathroom if you'd like."

"I appreciate that, but I have extra clothes at the station. I'll grab a shower and change there." He stuffed a biscuit loaded with honey in his mouth. "Wow, these are great," he mumbled around the tasty food.

Melanie tucked a strand of wayward hair behind her ear. A tinge of pink rose on her cheeks. "Thanks." She lowered her face and took a bite. The same piece of hair fell.

His hand twitched to move it back in place, but he kept his fingers wrapped around his coffee cup.

What was wrong with him? He had no business thinking romantic thoughts about the woman whose selfish act had destroyed his life. Melanie was guilty. The blame for Allison's death lay at her feet. If she'd only taken Allison with her, or had told the police what had happened. But no. Mel insisted she couldn't remember.

He shook his head. Nope. He didn't believe her. How could anyone forget what happened to their best friend?

The sheriff station's main room consisted of the reception counter, a waiting area and two desks. Melanie blinked. She'd remembered the Anderson County Sheriff's Department being small, but not this small.

Jason swooped his hand in an arch. "Welcome to ACSD."

Her jaw hung open. "Is this all of it?"

He chuckled. "No. The county renovated the building a few years ago, right after Dennis took over. This is the entrance. There are several offices, a supply room, an armory, the sheriff's office and a gym with locker rooms beyond that door over there." He pointed to a passageway on the far side of the room.

She exhaled. So she hadn't fallen into Mayberry. "Where will I be working?"

"Dennis...excuse me, I guess I should say Sheriff Monroe." Jason grinned. "He set you up with an office here at the station and a dedicated lab next door. Follow me. I'll give you a quick tour. Then I'll go change while you check out your new office digs."

She trailed behind him as he led her to the back part of the station.

Six offices, including Sheriff Monroe's, lined the hallway. Two for the four detectives on the force, an interrogation room, a soft interview room and one for her.

Her gaze landed on the door plaque. She ran her fingers across the gold-edged brown plastic nameplate.

Dr. Melanie Hutton, Forensic Anthropologist/County Coroner. She'd always shared a lab with her colleagues. Never had a room to herself. A sense of satisfaction filled her. She'd achieved her goal of becoming a forensic anthropologist. Her one-time dream of a counseling degree had disintegrated when Allison had disappeared. From that point on, finding her friend had consumed her life's path.

A jingle grabbed her attention.

Jason held out a ring of keys. "They must have added your name to the door this morning. I hadn't realized you had your PhD, Dr. Hutton."

Her shoulders drooped. "I'm just plain old Melanie, thank you very much." Her fingers brushed his as she accepted the key ring. She jerked away her hand, but not before a warm tingle danced up her arm. The teenage crush she'd hidden all those years ago rose to the surface. She tamped it down. The man had no interest in her. Never had, never would.

The key slid into the lock with a metallic click, and the door opened. As she peered inside, Melanie's jaw dropped. A large mahogany desk with an executive chair sat to the left. Two gorgeous burgundy leather seats placed in front of her work space created a professional but warm atmosphere.

"Will it be okay?" Jason's baritone voice broke her musing.

She turned to face him. "Excuse me?"

"The office. Is it adequate?"

"It's perfect." She had yet to figure out how the small department found funding for her position. Most law-enforcement departments contracted out services. Granted, Anderson County would have priority, but she'd contract out across the region when other counties needed a forensic anthropologist. However, to be employed by ACSD and not by a large lab was unusual, to say the least. And what about being appointed as county coroner? She hadn't applied. It had fallen in her lap. The whole situation seemed unreal.

"Come on. I'll show you the rest." He slipped back into professional mode and continued his tour.

A little farther down the hall, a break room with a black couch and 1950s retro table and chairs caught her attention. The quaint space had character. She wondered who in the department had the decorator's touch.

"Now I know where to find the coffee." She lingered in the doorway.

Jason nodded. "A very important commodity around here."

At the end of the passage, he opened the door to the gym. Not large, but it had all the equipment that a small department needed. Two locker rooms attached to the workout room had signs that read Men and Women. She breathed a sigh of relief. They had separate areas. She'd noticed several female deputies since arriving, and they all seemed happy with their jobs. Within a small town, you never knew how widespread the good-ol'-boys club might reach. Nice to know it hadn't tainted Valley Springs.

She peeked in the room labeled Women. Not huge, but more than sufficient. Two small rows of lockers and a bench seat in between, plus two showers and a bathroom area off to the side. Grateful for the space to clean up in, she made a mental note to bring an extra change of clothes to leave in the locker. With her job, she never knew when she'd be covered in dirt from head to toe.

"I'll let you go check out your new office while I grab a shower."

"Sure. Come find me when you're done." She strolled

back to her little slice of paradise and dropped into her office chair. Swinging back and forth in her seat, she smiled. Maybe returning home wouldn't come back to haunt her.

Several files sat in the middle of her desk. She flipped open the top one and scanned the documents. A coroner case. An elderly man passed away, and the family had concerns as to cause of death. She'd pull all the evidence later and take a look. She picked up the next file.

The evidence in a cold case stared back at her.

As she examined the first set of documents, the pictures of remains mentally took her to the grave. The bones spoke to her, begging her to solve the case.

"Who are you? And what happened to you?"

Showered and in clean jeans and a button-down shirt, Jason headed to Melanie's office. His mind struggled to come to grips with his inner turmoil. He'd hated her for fifteen years, but yesterday's events had him confused. Each time he looked at her, he remembered the sweet kid he'd known during his youth.

Leaning against the doorjamb, he watched as she studied the file in front of her and twirled a strand of hair between her fingers. So like the young girl he'd grown up with. Allison and Melanie had sat at the kitchen table every night and worked on homework together. They'd call him over when they required help. He hadn't minded the excuse to sit next to her.

During those years, he learned Melanie's look of concentration. Her head tilted to the left, and she'd twirl her hair. The narrowed gaze gave away the seriousness of her thinking. And right now, the woman was deep in thought.

Hand on his chest, he rubbed small circles in a desperate attempt to remove the pain of his sister's disappearance and Melanie's betrayal and departure. If only the simple movement had that power.

He cleared his throat.

Melanie jolted, sending papers flying off her desk. Hand over her mouth, her breaths came in quick gasps. "Jason."

He cringed. "I didn't mean to scare you."

"No. It's my fault. I get engrossed in my work, and the world could collapse around me, and I wouldn't know it." She scooped the papers into a pile.

Jason kneeled and collected the pictures that had fallen to the floor. He tapped them into a neat stack and handed them to her.

"Thanks."

He slipped in behind her and peered over her shoulder. Her coconut shampoo tapped into another memory from years past. She and Allison had loved coconut. Shampoos, lotions, candles—anything with the coconut scent. The aroma short-circuited his ability to think. Affection and anger warred in his brain.

He struck his knuckle next to the file. "That's an old one. Have any insights into the case?"

"A few." She sorted the documents and arranged them back into the proper order.

"Do tell."

"See this picture of the victim's ribs?" She placed a capped pen on the photo.

He shook off his conflicting emotions and squinted to where the end of her pen pointed. "What exactly am I looking at?"

"The direction of that bone. See how it angles up and toward the spine?"

Unable to discern what she had indicated, he leaned in. "You mean how it pushes in?"

"That's it. It might have happened after death, but it's in the perfect position to suggest a punctured lung."

He skirted the desk and slipped into one of her new easy chairs. Leaning back, he stretched out his legs and crossed his ankles. "Interesting find. I look forward to hearing your conclusions after a full examination of the evidence."

"Were the bones released for burial?" Melanie had sunk low in her seat. She propped her foot on the desk to elevate her ankle and twirled a strand of hair as she perused the file.

"No. He's still a John Doe. The county has them in storage."

"I'll pull them later when I have time and take a closer look after we exhume the remains I found yesterday. It's not like another few weeks will change this gentleman's situation."

A quick glance at his watch told him the early morning chill had burned off. "Speaking of which, I'm guessing you'd like to get to work at the grave site."

"If it's okay with you, I want to go out there as soon as possible."

"I don't see why we can't leave now." He sat up straight.

"Sounds good." She lowered her foot to the floor and eased herself to a standing position. After collecting the papers, she locked them in her file cabinet and pocketed the keys. "I'm ready."

He motioned to the door. "After you." He patted his side, confirming he'd holstered his weapon after his shower.

The last thing he wanted was for Melanie to be out in the open, but she had a job to do, and so did he—protecting her, in case her attacker tried again.

* * *

Dirt clung to Melanie's sweaty arms. She'd arrived at the burial site midmorning and had worked for six hours nonstop. Bathroom and water breaks being the only exceptions. The cool morning air had grown warmer, and she'd shed the top half of her coveralls, letting it hang from her waist, hours ago. It might be fifty degrees, but the winter sun beat down on her.

Thankful the ground hadn't frozen yet this season, she brushed soil from the skull she'd discovered twenty minutes ago. The yellow tarps held multiple bones, and the blue tarps acted as a collection center for the dirt from the exhumation.

Pen between her teeth, she scooped out the big find and added it to the assortment of bones. She picked up her clipboard and noted the location and item on the checklist. Brushing a strand of loose hair from her forehead with the back of her hand, she arched her spine. A series of cracks relieved the ache settling in the small of her back.

Climbing from the hole, she moved to the perimeter of the scene and grabbed another water from her personal cooler. She held the cold bottle to her neck and sighed with relief. Her body ached, and the heat from the sun irritated her scrapes and cuts. She leaned against a tree trunk and stared at the shallow grave. The three-foot burial depth had worked in her favor, shortening the duration of the job. She tilted back her head and filled her lungs. Another day and she'd spend her time in the lab, examining instead of exhuming.

If not for Jason and Keith tag-teaming protection duty throughout the day, she wouldn't have been able to focus. Who had targeted her and why continued to elude her. She appreciated the security and planned to tell Jason when she had a chance. It couldn't be easy for him. She knew he held her accountable for Allison's death, and she didn't blame him. With her fragmented memory, it made it impossible to defend her actions, even to herself. Her grip tightened, and the bottle crinkled in her hand. Allison begging her to go for help was one of the few clear moments in her brain. She'd left her friend. But it didn't matter that she'd led the deputies back to the cabin; Allison's body had disappeared and hadn't been found since. How could she ever release the guilt?

Sparrows chirped, and distant voices from the trail drifted in her direction. She tilted her head and gazed into the sky. White wisps of clouds floated above. Melanie inhaled the fresh air, something Dallas, Texas, hadn't possessed. The mixture of pain and joy from her childhood confused her. Could she handle living in Valley Springs? Maybe if her memory returned and removed all doubt as to what had happened, but until then, she'd trust God and muddle through the best she could.

She rolled her neck from side to side. The quandary would have to wait. She had a job to finish. She downed her drink and chucked the empty bottle into the red-and-white ice chest. It landed with a thump. Taking a step, she winced. The break in her work had tightened her muscles. Her ankle screamed at her, but so did the rest of her body. The ibuprofen she'd taken that morning had helped, but the effect had worn off a while ago. She'd call it a day in another couple of hours, but until then, she'd push forward. She dug her toe into the dirt and rolled her ankle in a circle, working out the stiffness.

"Does it still hurt?"

She jumped.

"Didn't mean to startle you. Guess I have a habit of doing that." Jason rested against the neighboring tree.

Several deep breaths later, she forced a smile. "It's okay."

He narrowed his gaze and studied her a moment. "Well? Does it?"

"A little." Truthfully, a lot, but Jason didn't need to know that. "I, uh, wanted to thank you for watching out for me today."

"Just doing my job." The muscles in his neck and shoulders tensed.

"We both know it's more than that." She wiped her hand down her face. "Jason. We're going to be working together for the foreseeable future. Do you think we can call a truce, at least while we do our jobs?"

His jaw twitched, and he remained silent.

She'd asked a lot, but the strain between them had to stop. She watched him for a few minutes then shook her head.

"Never mind." She pushed from the trunk and limped to the hole in the ground. Her lead-filled heart threatened to drop to her feet. To think that fifteen years ago, she'd had a crush on him. He'd teased her and Allison, but he'd never allowed others to speak unkind words to them. If only she could return to those carefree days. The days before she had died on the inside and her friend had died for real.

Someday, Allison, I'll find your body. I promise.

She swiped the wetness from her cheeks and lowered herself into the grave. The movement mimicked her mood. She picked up her trowel and searched for more bones.

An hour later, Melanie's headache had become unbearable, causing her stomach to roil. Just what she needed, to lose her lunch in front of Jason. Scanning the grave, she spotted the paintbrush she used for delicate work. She grasped the handle, but dropped it. She tried again, but her fingers refused to cooperate. Her eyelids grew heavy. Something was off. She sat on the edge of the hole.

"Jason, help." Her words were slurred. She struggled to stay upright. The trees in front of her blurred and swayed.

He kneeled down and came face-to-face with her. "What's wrong?"

"I don't know."

"Help me out here. What's the last thing you did?"

"I—I…" She struggled against the gray cloud jumbling her thoughts. "Took a break a while ago. Only digging since."

His gaze flew to a spot behind her.

She wilted into him. Her vision tunneled, and darkness closed in.

"Keith! Grab the cooler and her bag!"

Jason's frantic voice registered, but her body had shut down.

His warm arms lifted her. Her head bobbed and landed on his shoulder.

Her cheek bounced against his chest in cadence with the pounding of his feet on the path.

His rhythmic breathing was the last thing she heard before the world went dark.

The disinfectant Valley Springs General Hospital used churned Jason's stomach, and the voices of the doctors and nurses hammered in his ears.

By the time he'd arrived at his truck, Melanie had lost consciousness. Her breathing had become labored, and her skin ashen. He'd cradled her in his arms while Keith drove like a madman. He'd once again considered praying as his partner broke every speed limit on the way to the hospital.

Keith had notified the ER and called the station. At least one of them had thought to send a deputy to secure the scene.

He ran his fingers through his hair and paced the hall. The fluorescent lights buzzed overhead, and the clunk of the vending machine grated on his nerves.

"How's she doing?" Keith laid a hand on his shoulder.

Jason met his partner's gaze. "I have no idea. But she didn't look good when they took her back."

"Have any idea what happened?"

"Not really." He twisted his mouth to the side. "Unless some critter in the dirt bit her, it had to be something she ingested."

Keith tapped his upper lip. "That's why you had me bring the cooler."

"I was grasping at possibilities. Figured the cooler, or maybe something in her bag, had caused the reaction."

"Come on. Let's get a cup of coffee and have a seat while we wait."

He followed Keith to the waiting room and plopped down on a blue plastic chair.

"Here." His friend handed him a paper cup of strong coffee. Keith sat next to him and rested his arms on his knees. "She means something to you, doesn't she?"

"Not hardly." At least not anymore. Maybe a long time ago he'd secretly liked her, but a twenty-year-old interested in a sixteen-year-old had *bad idea* written all over it.

"I don't buy it. What happened between you two?"

"Melanie was my sister's best friend. They did everything together. Even planned to go to the same college when they graduated. But that never happened. Well, not for my sister, anyway."

Keith pursed his lips. "She's one of our cold cases, right?"

Jason nodded and swallowed past the lump in his throat. Yes, Allie was a cold case, but the term sounded sterile. His sister had been vibrant and full of life. Until that night.

"Wait." Keith's jaw dropped. "Melanie's the *other* girl."

"Yes." The old anger bubbled to the surface. "She escaped and left Allison with the man who'd abducted them."

His partner scratched his chin. "From what I've read, it's amazing she got out."

"Yeah, right. What about what she did to Allie?" He clenched his fist.

"Have you actually asked her about it?"

"I don't need—"

"Detective Cooper?" The doctor was standing in the doorway.

"Right here." Jason rose and met the doctor. "How is she?"

"She's resting quietly. She should make a full recovery."

He exhaled. If he and God were on speaking terms, he'd send up a big thank-you.

"It's a good thing you brought the cooler with you."

Jason tilted his head. "Why? What was it?"

"She was poisoned with antifreeze. We found it on the threads of two water bottles." The doctor ran a hand over the back of his neck. "She's a fortunate lady. We treated her with fomepizole. It should counter the effects within the next three hours."

Poisoned? He'd had Keith grab the cooler only as a precaution.

"You're welcome to go on back. Ms. Hutton is in room two-oh-three. Just don't bother her. She needs her rest."

"Thanks." Jason's mind spun around the word *anti-freeze*. Not something they'd normally come across.

"You're welcome." The doctor patted Jason's upper arm and turned to leave.

"Hey, doc?"

The man glanced at him over his shoulder.

"How long will she be here?"

"If all goes well, she'll be released in a couple of days." With his answer given, the doctor went back to work.

"You want first or second?" Keith crumpled his coffee cup in a ball and chucked it in the trash.

"What?" Jason blinked. Had he missed part of a conversation?

"Figure she needs a guard on her door. Was asking which shift you wanted."

"Oh. Yeah, guess we should do that. I'll take first." Jason's head swirled with the doctor's news. When had someone tampered with her water bottles? Had he let down his guard and missed the creep messing with her drinks?

"Dude. For someone who doesn't mean anything to you, you sure are out of sorts."

What could he say to that? Keith was right about one thing. He had to get his head in the game, or it might cost Melanie her life.

"I'll check in with security and then swing by one more time before relieving you in six hours." Keith smacked him on the back and sauntered away.

Jason's stomach knotted. He'd left Melanie alone for far too long. Determined that no one would hurt her on his watch, Jason hurried to her room and pushed open the door. His breath caught at the sight of her. She looked so young. Not like the capable woman who'd burst into his life and taken over the crime scene yesterday.

Brown hair fanned out over the pillow. Her face had a tinge of pink, but dark circles under her eyes stood out like neon signs. He scanned her form under the blanket. He'd never realized how petite she was. Her bigger-than-life personality had always outweighed her size.

Memories swamped him from his younger years. Melanie and Allison had become inseparable in elementary school. A close friendship they'd kept until the day they disappeared. He'd enjoyed teasing them, especially when they hit junior high and high school. He'd bug them until the two doubled over in tears from giggling so hard. Truth be told, he missed hearing Melanie's laugh.

Soft beeps of the heart monitor jerked him out of the past. He wanted to find that Melanie again. The one who made him smile. Not the Melanie who'd ripped out his heart. He missed his sister so much.

Jason had pored over the police files of their abduction a hundred times since joining the sheriff's department, searching for a clue. Any clue. The police department had called in help from surrounding counties and had done a wide search for two days after the girls had disappeared. Jason had been the last one to see them alive. One minute they'd sat at the kitchen table doing their homework, and the next they were gone. After over twenty interviews of townspeople coming to relay what they thought might be helpful, the police had nothing. Until Melanie showed up beaten and traumatized. Without his sister.

He wandered to Melanie's bedside and gripped the metal rail. Leaning in, he whispered, "Why did you leave her?"

Silence met his question.

His gut twisted. All this time, his anger had taken a front-row seat, but now, looking at Melanie, he couldn't reconcile the fierce friend she'd been and the coward she'd become that night. It didn't make sense.

Her rhythmic breathing calmed him. He'd stuff the past into the background and focus on the here and now. And right now, Melanie needed him. He hadn't forgiven her—no, that wouldn't happen—but her life depended on him setting aside his resentment until he caught her attacker.

He tucked the white blanket around her, then pulled the tan easy chair beside the bed. Resting his head on the back of the seat, he stared at the ceiling.

"Don't worry, Allie. I'm going to find out who hurt you if it's the last thing I do." He swallowed past the lump that had taken up residence in his throat. "I miss you, sis."

His sister would want him to watch over Melanie, maybe even forgive her, but he couldn't do that. Not now, maybe not ever.

Fatigue draped over him like a cloak. After sleeping in his truck last night, he should have asked Keith to take the first shift so he could grab a few hours of shut-eye. He scrubbed his face with his hands, fighting his heavy eyelids to stay open. His eyes closed of their own accord.

Vivid images of Allison haunted his dreams.

Little men with jackhammers pounded on Melanie's brain. Grit cemented her eyelids closed, and a desert had inhabited her mouth.

Her ears, on the other hand, worked just fine. Jason's confession nearly broke her heart. *I miss her, too, Jason.*

She longed for the days when the three of them used to hang out and watch movies together at the Cooper house.

After listening to Jason's one-sided conversation with Allison, she soon heard soft snores from beside her. She struggled to open her eyes. When she finally pried them open, she shifted her gaze to him.

He'd propped his feet on the bed frame and crossed his arms. His chin rested against his chest. Even in his sleep, the man exuded strength.

A smile tugged on her lips, then fell. She'd been his sister's best friend, and over the years, they'd forged a bond beyond simple friendship. His and Allie's mom had died of cancer when he was sixteen, and Melanie had grieved with them. So, when he'd yelled at her after the deputies hadn't found Allison's body and then walked away from her, her world had imploded. The loss of her best friend, her parents' betrayal and his father's silence, along with Jason's lack of belief in her made for the perfect storm. Why hadn't he listened to her and tried to understand? She'd needed him. She'd had enough guilt to last a lifetime. His rejection had only amplified the pain.

The door whooshed open, and the tall figure of a male nurse appeared. His gaze darted around the room and landed on Jason.

"Sorry. I'll only be a minute," the nurse whispered. Shadows, along with a medical mask, obscured his face.

She nodded and kept her attention on the man beside her bed. Her heart leaped. Maybe Jason had put aside his animosity. He'd stayed by her side, hadn't he?

God, I know it's a lot to ask, but could You please chip away at his resentment? I want my friend back.

The nurse pulled a syringe from a bowl.

"This should help."

Help with what? Her headache? Her gaze met the nurse's. Black soulless eyes glared back at her. She'd seen them before, during her attack in the woods.

"No!" she croaked. She yanked out her IV before he inserted the needle and pushed down the plunger, knocking the nurses' station call remote onto the floor. It clattered on the tiles. "Jason!" The strangled plea tore from her lips.

Boots slapped on the ground. Jason bolted from his seat. "Melan…" She heard him gasp. "Hey!" He lowered his shoulder and tackled the assailant, slamming the man to the wall.

Grunts and smacks against flesh turned Melanie's stomach.

She scrambled to the floor and crouched behind the bed. *Lord, protect him.*

The fake nurse scrambled away, picked up a lamp and bashed Jason in the head.

Jason collapsed with a thud.

Melanie screamed and prayed someone heard the commotion.

After a quick glance in her direction, the attacker snarled then sprinted from the room.

Melanie crawled across the floor to Jason's side. She pulled him onto her lap and smoothed his hair from his forehead. "Please wake up." Tears rolled down her face and off her chin. If Jason lost his life because of her, she'd never forgive herself.

Footsteps sent her pulse racing. She searched for a weapon within reach but found nothing to defend herself and Jason.

An imposing figure stood in the doorway, blocking the hall light. "Jason? Melanie?"

Relief flooded her. "Keith, help." A whimper escaped her lips.

"What happened?" Jason's partner kneeled and surveyed the scene.

"A guy dressed as a nurse attacked me. Jason tried to stop him."

He pointed to Jason. "You've got him?"

"Yes. Go." She sucked in a ragged breath as Keith sprinted from the room.

Voices streamed in from the hall and the IV machine's sharp alarm registered in her brain. How long had the warning been going off?

She struggled to pray, but the words wouldn't come. Her chin dropped to her chest. God knew what she needed. She'd leave it up to Him.

A nurse dashed in and took in the scene. The upended items in the room had to be quite the sight. Janie, according to the woman's name tag, kneeled next to Melanie.

"How ya doin', sweetie?"

"I'm okay. But I'm not so sure about him." Melanie gestured toward the man in her lap.

Jason roused and moaned. His eyes fluttered open. He grimaced. "Are you okay?"

"Me? It's you I'm worried about."

"I have a splitting headache, but I'll live." He struggled to an upright position and clutched his head.

"Take it easy, hon. That's a nasty lump." Janie examined his head. "You need a CT scan. I'll get—"

"No. I'm fine."

The nurse jammed a fist on her hip and scowled.

"I promise. I'm good."

Janie pointed to Jason. "No, you're not, but I can't force you."

He closed his eyes and released a puff of air through pursed lips. When he opened his eyes, he gaped at Melanie's arm. "You're bleeding."

She hadn't noticed the crimson liquid dripping from her hand. Her thoughts had centered on Jason when she'd witnessed him going down. "I yanked out my IV, that's all. He put something in the port. I didn't want to wait and see what happened."

"Makes sense." Jason staggered to his feet and swayed. Janie grabbed one arm, and he placed his other hand on the wall to steady himself.

Melanie bit her lower lip. "Maybe you should rest for a bit longer." The man looked a little green around the edges. "I'm good."

Doubtful, but she knew him well enough that talking him into sitting down would be impossible.

"Stubborn man," Janie muttered. She moved to Melanie's side and helped her into bed. The nurse threw a towel on the floor to soak up the fluids, then inserted a new IV and hung a new bag. "There ya go, honey. If you need anything else, let me know."

Jason straightened but hadn't removed his hand from the wall. "We'll need that tubing as evidence. I want to know what that man put in it."

"No problem, Detective." Janie grabbed a plastic bag from a drawer and slipped the tubing inside. "I'll leave it here on the nightstand for your partner."

"Thanks." Jason swallowed. "I appreciate it."

The woman patted Melanie's leg. "Let me know if you need anything else. And try to convince Mr. I'm Fine to let the doctor look him over."

The corners of Melanie's mouth lifted. "I'll try."

Janie shook her head, then pointed at Jason. "I'll go get you an ice pack." She slipped past him and exited the room.

Jason hung his head. "I need to search the hospital."

"Keith's already looking." Melanie gestured toward the chair. "You don't look so hot. Sit down before you fall down."

"Thanks a lot." He quirked a lopsided smile and winced.

His swollen jaw and red eye made her flinch. Poor guy would have a nice shiner by tomorrow. The man had to be hurting after the wallop he'd received, but she'd take his attempted smile. Any step toward civility was progress.

Jason released the wall and swayed.

Keith rushed into the room, his gaze landing on Jason. "Whoa there, partner." He extended his hand.

Jason waved him off and straightened. "Find the slime bag?"

"Afraid not. I'll check with security and go through the video. See if we can identify the creep."

Jason ambled to Melanie's side on unsteady feet. "Go. Check the camera footage. I can handle things here. Oh, and take the IV tubing to the lab."

"I'm on it." Keith grabbed the plastic bag and hurried from the room.

Jason lowered himself onto the cushioned chair and gingerly touched his cheekbone. His gaze shifted to her. "Get some rest. I promise not to fall asleep this time." An expression of self-recrimination flashed across his face.

"Don't." She refused to allow him to blame himself. He'd been with her every step of the way, even though he'd been infuriated with her due to her role in his sister's disappearance. Why had her memory continued to hide? She wanted to reach into her brain and scoop out the information. She'd loved Allison like a sister. She recalled Allie begging her to go get help, but why had she escaped and not taken Allie with her?

"I should go and let someone else stay. I should never have fallen asleep. My job was to keep you safe. I failed."

"No, you didn't. You protected me. I'm alive because of you."

He huffed and crossed his arms over his chest. "I'll

agree to disagree if you'll get some rest." His body had recovered enough that he'd gained back his tenacity.

"Only if you stay with me." She watched him fight an internal battle and waited for him to reply. "Jason."

His gaze met hers.

"You're the only person I trust." Unsure how he'd respond, she held her breath. But she had to be honest with him. Everyone who'd accepted her for who she was had died, except for him. He might dislike her, but he was all she had left in this world.

"All right, Mel, you win." He called Keith on his cell phone. "When you're done with the video, consider yourself on duty." He pursed his lips as he listened. "Thanks for having my back…got it. Will do." Jason ended the call and returned his focus to her. "I am sorry."

"Please don't beat yourself up. I'm grateful for all you've done."

His lips in a thin line, he nodded and dimmed the lights on her remote. "Go to sleep. You'll need your energy for tomorrow if you plan to break out of this joint."

She smiled at his attempt to play nice and followed his directions.

But sleep didn't come easy. And even in her dreams, the man who'd attacked her came after her. She had no way of stopping him, in her dreams or in real life.

The knowledge that Keith stood guard outside Melanie's room allowed Jason to breathe easier. He wanted to smack himself for falling asleep. He'd let her down. Since he'd found her darting through the woods, he'd appointed himself her personal bodyguard. Why he'd done that continued to baffle him. She'd hurt him deeply, and yet he'd refused to let her fend for herself. And the crazy thing was, the longer he stayed at her side, the harder holding on to his anger had become.

His gaze drifted to her. She laid on her side, facing him, hands pressed together under her cheek. How many times had her youthful, innocent appearance startled him since she'd arrived? Yes, she was four years younger than his thirty-five, but life after Allie had aged him. He'd become the proverbial grumpy old man. Something his friend and boss, Dennis, often pointed out.

He shifted his aching body and bit back a groan. The bold man who'd entered Melanie's room had done a number on his head and muscles. Jason replayed the events in his mind. A familiarity plagued him. There was something about the man's build that toyed with his brain. Who had he wrestled with? *Is this how Melanie feels when she tries to remember?* If it was, he now had a better understanding of her frustration. He rested his head on the back of the chair and processed the new information.

True to her word, the nurse had brought him an ice pack, which had helped, but the bag, now lukewarm, sat on the roller table. He wanted to request another one, but that required movement on his part. The concept of standing made him cringe. No, he'd stay right where he was.

A few hours later, the early morning sun streamed through the blinds, rousing him from a light sleep. He awoke to find Melanie curled on her side, her sable brown eyes peering at him.

"Morning." He pushed himself to a sitting position. His muscles had stiffened, and every bump and bruise throbbed. He hadn't smarted this bad since Allison and Melanie dared him to run that stupid obstacle race when he was eighteen. What had he been thinking? Impressing Melanie, that's what. But that was then, and this was now. Now, they were practically strangers. Except not.

He shook off his confusion. Wow, that man had hit him harder than he'd thought.

"Good morning." She gave him a lazy smile.

A knock at the door had him sliding his hand to his Glock.

"Well, well, Prince Charming finally woke up." Keith entered, holding a breakfast tray.

The aroma of bacon and eggs wafted across the room. Jason's stomach growled. "Sorry."

"Sounds like someone's hungry." Melanie adjusted the bed to an upright position.

"My partner is always hungry." Keith slid the tray onto the roller table, grabbed a strip of bacon and shoved it in his mouth. "I got everything from the cafeteria, so no worries about the food being tampered with."

Jason lost his appetite. The idea of someone poisoning her meal turned his gut.

"You okay there, dude?" Keith squinted at him.

"Yeah." His partner had saved his hide once again. Self-recrimination blanketed him. He'd lost his ability to think clearly, and if he didn't get his head on straight, Melanie could lose her life.

Keith leaned in and whispered, "Relax. Only one of us has to think about it."

"Right." But that didn't keep the guilt from latching on like a dog with a bone.

"Come on, guys. Let's eat." Melanie's gaze darted between him and his partner. "I'd like to get out of here."

He lifted an eyebrow. "Don't you think it's wise to wait a bit longer?" He already knew her answer.

"No. I hate hospitals. I'm not staying." She dove into her breakfast with a little too much gusto.

The woman had plenty of reasons to detest hospitals. He'd help her escape, but with one stipulation. "I'll help and give you a ride on one condition. You agree to protection."

She opened her mouth to respond, but he stopped her.

"No argument. Take it or leave it."

"All right, you win."

He hadn't wanted to win. He wanted Melanie safe. And the only way to achieve that goal was to keep her close.

Her attacker had crossed a line last night. The man had proven that he'd go to any lengths to get at Melanie.

Jason refused to let that happen.

FOUR

The passenger window of Jason's truck cooled the side of Melanie's face. Her body ached and head hurt, but she refused to spend another minute at the hospital. Jason had supported her desire to leave and offered her a ride. She hadn't planned on his insistence that she stay in his guest room. Adamant that her safety depended on it, he wouldn't take no for an answer.

What choice did she have? No one else cared enough to protect her. Her parents had told her not to speak of her trauma—to just get over it. Their concern about reputation had severed their already flimsy relationship. She'd fled to her aunt Heather's, where she stayed until college. When her aunt passed away, she had no one in her life who cared enough to look out for her. Except Jason… but why did he care? Melanie's temples throbbed harder.

She sensed his anger simmering under the surface multiple times since she'd arrived in Valley Springs. But, so far, he'd held it at bay, she'd give him that.

The truck slowed to a stop. Jason draped his wrist over the steering wheel while waiting for the light to turn green. "You sure you're okay?"

"I'm good. Just tired." After the lack of sleep last night, she craved a nap. "You know, you can drop me off at my place and go on home. You don't have to baby-sit me."

His eyebrows rose to his hairline. "You're kidding, right? You were attacked twice, not to mention the person who watched your apartment two nights ago. If it's all the same to you, I don't want your death on my conscience."

Ouch. That hurt.

The guilt from leaving Allie behind, and the simple fact that she'd survived when her friend had died, sent daggers piercing her heart. She wanted to scream at Jason. Why hadn't he listened? Allison had begged her to go for help. Of that, she was sure. She opened her mouth, then shut it. No sense in starting that particular argument, especially since everything else about those two days in captivity remained a mystery.

"I…" He huffed and accelerated through the intersection when the light changed.

The bare trees dotting the edge of the street reminded her of her own life. Sad, lonely and lifeless. All she had left in her world was her job. And God. If Aunt Heather hadn't taken her in and pointed her to the Heavenly Father who loved her unconditionally, where would she be right now? She shook off the melancholy thoughts and shifted her attention to Jason. "I appreciate your willingness to watch out for me."

He shrugged. "We'll stop at your apartment and pick up some clothes and whatever else you need. Then I'll take you to my house. I bought the old Evans place about five years ago. So there's plenty of room. I have two guest rooms along with an office."

His dismissal of her comment stung. But what had she expected? That he'd welcome her with open arms? She turned to stare out the window as they reached the town square. The flurry of the lunchtime crowd reminded her of ants on their way to a picnic. Leafless trees whipped by as Jason neared her address at the far end of the business district.

"I always loved that house. Mrs. Evans used to invite me over for tea parties when I was little. She made the best cookies. And Mr. Evans built that cool treehouse for us kids to play in. Remember that?"

"Remember it?" He chuckled. "It's still there. I fixed it up soon after I moved in."

She pivoted and faced him. "Are you serious?"

"Serious as a heart attack." He pulled into a parking spot near her building.

She opened the passenger door and slipped from the seat. The abandoned store below her apartment had never concerned her. In fact, the idea of solitude appealed to her. No customers coming and going, no owner puttering around early in the morning or late at night. Today, the emptiness twisted her stomach into a pretzel.

Jason fell into step beside her.

"It won't take me long. I don't have much stuff to start with." She took the stairs up to her new home. When she'd moved in, the outdoor entrance on the second floor had bothered her, but today gratitude filled her. No place for an intruder to hide and wait.

Each step zapped her energy, and her ankle protested the movements, but she powered on. She didn't want Jason to see her vulnerable. But she *was* weak and hated that fact. She considered the thoughts rolling around in her mind and bit her lip.

God, I'm sorry for my prideful thoughts. Help me accept the support and protection I need. Don't let my stubbornness get in the way.

She glanced over her shoulder at the man who had put aside his resentment to be there for her.

Jason ran his hand up the rail as he followed her. "So you moved in a few days ago?"

"Yup." She inserted her key and opened the door. "Welcome back to my humble abode."

He stepped inside, no doubt focusing on her small stack of unpacked boxes along the wall. "Are you sending for the rest of your things later?"

She latched the door behind her and shifted her gaze to meet his. "No. This is it. I don't have anything else."

His eyebrows rose.

"Don't need much. When you don't have many friends or family, you tend to move around a lot." Why had she opened her big mouth?

"Never put down roots anywhere?"

She stepped to the small table by the entrance and dropped her keys into the crystal bowl her aunt had given her. One of her few treasured possessions. "Nope."

Jason surveyed the living room then peeked into the kitchen. "Can I help with anything?"

"Have a seat. I'll go pack a bag and be right out." Melanie hurried to her bedroom to escape his questions.

She closed the door and leaned against the wooden barrier. She never should have admitted to being alone in this world. Now he'd pity her. Assuming he'd ever get over the anger that continued to grip him.

She pushed off the door and flung open her closet. The door screeched and bounced on its hinges. *Relax, girl. The closet isn't your enemy.* Inhaling a calming breath, she stretched to grab her duffel and flinched. Pain shot through her torso. Not a place on her body didn't ache. With more care, she pulled the bag from the top shelf and set it on the bed.

After changing, she tossed in a pair of sweatpants, along with T-shirts and sweatshirts from her dresser, she returned to the closet and chose several outfits that met her work needs. She glanced at the short row of shoes on the floor. Tennis shoes and work boots would suffice, but her fleece-lined boots beckoned her. What would it hurt to throw those in, too? Her gut told her comfort items would be a necessity in the days to come.

Her toiletries remained unpacked, so she grabbed her cosmetic case and stuffed it into the duffel, then zipped the bag closed. Hefting it on her shoulder, she staggered against the weight on her bruised and battered body. After one last scan of her bedroom, she returned to the living room.

Jason approached, took the duffel from her and stepped toward the door.

Normally, she'd insist on carrying her own things, but too tired and too sore to care, she accepted his help.

His hand on the knob, he turned. "Is that everything?"

"Thanks for lugging my heavy bag." She bit her lip and turned in a slow circle. "I think that's all I need." She'd forgotten something, but what? She snapped her fingers. The picture. "I need to grab one more thing. I'll meet you at the truck."

"Don't take too long." He stepped out and closed the door. His footfalls echoed as he trotted down the stairs.

Melanie slipped into her room and plopped on the side of the bed. A five-by-seven picture frame graced her nightstand. She and her childhood best friend stood, arms over each other's shoulders, grinning at the camera. If her memory served her correctly, Jason had taken the photo after the two of them had returned from their first high-school softball game.

Tears welled in her eyes. *Oh, Allison.* She clutched the picture and hugged it to her chest. Curling up on her bed, she let the sorrow flow.

* * *

Jason's heart warmed at the sight of the town's favorite lady, Mrs. Evans. She had the ear of the community and eyes everywhere. No one made a move without her knowing about it.

"Hi, Mrs. Evans. How are you today?" Jason placed Melanie's duffel in the back seat of his truck and slammed the door shut.

"Well, hello, young man. I'm as good as can be expected for someone with one foot in the grave." The older woman cackled.

"You do not have one foot in the grave. You're the spunkiest eighty-year-old I know."

"Ha. I'm one of the only eighty-year-olds you know." She patted the side of his face. "But I love you for the nice thought."

He clasped Judith Evans's paper-thin hand and kissed her cheek. "You're a treasure. Let me know if you need anything. I'm glad to help."

"I will, honey." Judith's gaze drifted to the second floor of the building. "You moving in? I thought you were happy with my old place."

"No, not moving. Melanie Hutton is renting the apartment. She had a rough couple of days, so I'm taking care of her."

The older lady smiled. "I always liked that girl. Too bad about her parents not wanting her after she and your sister were kidnapped."

Not wanting her? When had that happened? "Mrs. Evans, what are you talking about? I know that they had a falling-out."

"It was more than that, hon. Those good-for-nothing parents of hers refused to get her into therapy. Said she needed to buck up and deal with it," she said, then tsked.

"Why on earth would they do that?" He knew her parents hadn't been supportive and had ignored her growing up, but what Mrs. Evans suggested was flat-out cruel.

"I've known those two since they were married. They always worried about two things. Money and what people thought. When Melanie struggled with her trauma, they were afraid their reputations would be ruined if their daughter appeared weak."

He rubbed the back of his neck. "I never knew that."

"Your sister was gone, and you were dealing with your own grief. That poor child had no one to lean on. Thank the Lord for her aunt. That wonderful lady saved sweet Melanie's life." She squeezed his hand. "Now, this old lady needs to get moving. I stayed too long at the church, helping Pastor Adam. It's a bit cold out here for these old bones. Besides, Harold will be awake from his afternoon nap and wonder where I disappeared to."

A smile tugged at his lips. So stubborn Mrs. Evans was giving Harold a run for his money.

Judith had lost her husband ten years ago. Eight years had passed when she'd announced that she'd placed herself back on the market. Ever since that day, the older generation of men had flocked in her direction. Harold, the town's most eligible bachelor at the retirement home, had a thing for Judith. "Finally giving Harold the time of day?"

"I'm letting him think I'm not interested. Best way for a girl to get a guy to notice her." She winked at Jason. "Now, you go take care of my Melanie. Tell her I said hello, and I expect a visit soon." Judith continued her two-block stroll back to the senior living apartments.

The older woman's words swirled in his brain. Parents were supposed to love and support children, not reject them. Of course, his own father had become a drunk since his sister's disappearance, and Jason had become Ben Cooper's caretaker. But he'd never doubted his father's love for him.

Jason checked his watch. What had detained Melanie? No one had entered her apartment. Even while chatting with Mrs. Evans, he'd been vigilant. But still…had he missed something?

He scanned the neighborhood and tensed. A blue sedan stopped next to Mrs. Evans. Judith shuffled to the passenger window and leaned in. With all that had happened recently, Jason was on edge. He squinted, attempting to ID the driver. The air whooshed from his lungs, and he relaxed when he realized it was his friend Tim's wife, Laney. Once his heart rate settled, he continued his survey of the area.

Not seeing anything out of place, he bounded up the steps and entered her apartment.

"Mel? Everything okay?" He wandered down the hall and knocked softly on her bedroom door. "Mel?" Cracking the door open, he peered in.

There on the bed, his childhood friend was curled up, sound asleep, snuggling a picture frame. He tiptoed in and gently removed the photo. Placing it on the nightstand, his breath caught. His sister's face beamed back at him. He rubbed his chest in hopes of eliminating the pain.

His gaze drifted to Melanie. Exhaustion had taken its toll. He snatched a throw blanket from the end of the bed and pulled it over her. He'd let her rest, then take her home once she woke.

Heavy-hearted, he made his way to the living room. He glanced around the space. Only one door. If he lied down and slept for a bit, he'd hear if anyone entered.

He eyed the couch. Not exactly the most comfortable sleeping arrangement, but it would do. A nap sounded like a wonderful idea. The ability to rest after the attack at the hospital had eluded him. He'd dozed for brief periods throughout the night, but the guilt had weighed heavy on his conscience and sleep had refused to come.

After flipping the lock and checking the windows, he moved to the sofa and plopped down. His headache had dulled, but his bruises remained tender. He scrubbed his face with his hands. A little rest would do him good.

With a quick tug, the afghan on the top of the couch tumbled down. Jason stretched out the best he could and pulled the blanket over him. His lids drooped, and sleep dragged him under.

Smoke tickled Jason's nose. He coughed and coughed again. His eyes fluttered open. A haze greeted him. He covered his nose and mouth with his T-shirt. Had something clogged the flue on his chimney? He flung his legs over the side of the couch and blinked. Tears filled his eyes, and the burning sensation intensified.

A scan of the room reminded him he hadn't fallen asleep at home, but in Melanie's apartment, and she didn't have a fireplace.

Flames dancing along the far wall grabbed his attention. He gasped and immediately regretted it as he choked on the foul air. He swiped his eyes and focused on the cause. Fire had engulfed the front door and spread outward, igniting Melanie's boxes. His pulse sped to an alarming rate.

He searched for a secondary exit, but one didn't exist. The only way out—not an option. He had to get Melanie out. Somehow. Keeping his nose and mouth covered, he sprinted to her room and threw the door open.

"Mel! Wake up!" He slammed the door shut and

rushed to her side. "Come on, Mel. We have to get out of here."

Wide brown eyes stared at him. She shot up. "What's wrong?"

"The apartment's on fire. The entrance is blocked. Is there another way out?"

Gray wisps filtered under the door. Returning to the living room was no longer possible. The bedroom window loomed as the only exit.

She coughed. "Escape ladder. Under the bed." She dropped to her knees, pulled out the red box and shoved it at him. "Here!" Melanie scooped up her throw blanket and crawled to the doorway.

He grabbed the container and popped open the latch while she stuffed the cloth in the gap under the door.

Working in tandem, they opened the window and hefted the ladder to the opening.

Jason attached the hooks. "I've got these. Drop the rungs."

She squeezed beside him and released the string ties. The metal clanged against the exterior of the building.

Hand out to assist her, he jutted his chin to the escape route. "You first." Thankfully, she didn't protest and accepted his help. The last thing he wanted was to waste time arguing.

Crawling over the edge, she eased herself onto the ladder. She hung onto the rungs and gazed up at him. "You better be right behind me."

"Trust me. I'm not staying a second longer than I have to." Sweat trickled down his back. Heat prickled his neck and arms. At the rate the temperature had risen in the last two minutes, he worried that if Melanie's injuries slowed her descent, he'd never make it out alive.

She nodded and focused on her task. Her climbing

rhythm exhibited an uneven gait. She favored her right ankle, and her tentative grip slowed her, but she pushed on.

Come on, Mel, hurry up. It's getting hot in here. He stuck his head out the window as far as possible and sucked in the cool air.

Death by fire—he never thought his life would end that way. The worst part was, if he succumbed to the blaze, who would keep Melanie safe? His heart pounded. He had to survive. At one time in his life, he would've prayed for help, but God hadn't listened then, so why would He listen now?

The ladder jiggled on the side of the building, tearing him from his morbid thoughts. He peered down.

Melanie's hand shielded her eyes as she stared up at him. "Jason! Get down here!"

A quick glance over his shoulder had his heart racing. A smoke ceiling had begun to form. He had a minute, two tops, before the fire killed him. He had to get out…now. He swung his leg over the windowsill and straddled the frame.

A crack vibrated the room. The bedroom door exploded inward.

Jason's arm flew over his head, and he ducked. The blistering heat whooshed toward him.

Fire had eaten its way through the apartment. Flames reached out like tentacles determined to grab him.

He flung himself out the window and scrambled to secure his grip on the ladder. He hoped he'd survive the fall if the hooks gave way. Two stories didn't necessarily mean death, but he had no intention of finding out how many bones he'd break. Speed was of the essence.

Foot, foot, hand, hand. He concentrated on the cadence. The fire crackled above. Unable to help himself, he glanced up, closing one eye to protect himself from the embers spitting down. Flames licked the upper part of the window. The heat stung the bare skin on his arms. He swallowed hard and increased his pace. At the bottom rung, he jumped the final bone-jarring five feet.

Melanie grabbed his arm and yanked him away from the building.

The escape ladder tumbled to the ground and crashed behind them. Jason's steps faltered at the realization of how close he'd come to falling. Recovering his balance, he clutched Melanie's hand and hurried away from the deadly blaze.

Safe on the other side of the street, he pivoted to face her.

Tears trailed her soot-stained face. Her clothes hadn't fared any better. Black smudges covered her navy blue state-university sweatshirt and leggings.

"Come here." He wrapped his arms around her and tugged her close.

Her sobs came hard and fast.

In that moment, his resentment faded, and nothing else mattered. He glanced at the blackened entryway. Burn marks marred the outside of the door. His heart hammered in his chest. If he hadn't woken when he had, they'd both be dead. The fire had ignited Melanie's boxes and moved at a rapid speed. The heat had become unbearable incredibly fast. He doubted the fire had been an accident. Had someone committed arson with the intent to kill?

The truth knocked the wind from him. They'd almost been burned alive.

"I'm sorry, Mel. I'll help you replace your stuff." He nuzzled his face into her smoke-laden hair. "Please, don't be sad." For a moment, he traveled back twenty years.

He'd said the same thing to her when her hamster died. He would've given her anything to stop her tears back then. Just as now, he wanted to make it all go away.

"I don't—didn't—have much to start with. I couldn't care less about the stuff. Except Aunt Heather's antique bowl." Her words were muffled against his shoulder.

"Then tell me what the sobbing's about." Tears were normal, but this went beyond a crying jag.

"I could have lost you."

His heart stopped. Had Melanie realized what she'd said? And when was the last time a woman had concerned herself with him? Any other woman, he'd explore his curiosity, but the past continued to flash like a neon sign in his brain. If it hadn't been for the near-death experience, he'd step back, but he needed the comfort as much as she did right now.

He smoothed a hand down her hair. "I'm right here. I'm not going anywhere."

Her body quit shaking, and she pulled away. She wiped the wetness with the heel of her hand, streaking black across her cheek.

Firetrucks arrived on the scene and sprayed water on the side of the building next to the alley. Protecting the adjacent building took priority over the vacant store and Melanie's apartment. It didn't matter. The fire had destroyed the structure beyond repair, consuming her possessions, as well.

Red and orange tendrils reached into the sky, mesmerizing and terrifying Jason as he sat with Melanie on the curb and watched as her new home went up in flames.

The fire captain, Phillip Scott, ambled toward them. His unbuckled turnout coat hung at an odd angle, revealing his sweat-stained VSFD T-shirt. The man's frazzled appearance told Jason all he needed to know.

Jason pressed his hands on the concrete to push himself to his feet.

The fireman waved him down. "Don't get up."

He sighed and placed his forearms on his knees. "It's arson, isn't it?"

"I was about to ask you that." The captain rubbed the back of his neck.

"That's my guess. Someone purposely blocked our exit. We were fortunate to get out alive."

"I noticed the escape ladder. Smart woman." The fire captain's gaze met Melanie's.

She nodded but remained quiet.

"Once the building cools, we'll start the official investigation. I'll let you know what we find." The man turned to leave and stopped. His focus returned to Melanie. "You know of anyone who'd want to hurt you?"

A dry laugh lingered in the air as she stared at what remained of her apartment.

"I'll take that as a yes. Cooper, I hope you're sticking close to protect her." Scott pinned him with a scowl.

"Yes, sir. I am." Assuming she wanted his help. He'd already failed twice—three times if you included the antifreeze poisoning, which he did.

"I'll send the paramedics over to check you two out. Smoke inhalation is nothing to mess with." The man jutted his chin toward Jason's red arms. "They should take a look at those burns, as well." Jason watched the captain make his way back to his men.

Brent and Ethan swaggered toward him, first-aid duffels hanging from their shoulders.

"Heard you were caught in that inferno over there." Brent jammed his thumb toward the burning building.

"You heard right. Not something I ever want to repeat. Your buddies are nuts running into those ovens."

Ethan snorted. "About as crazy as you dodging bullets."

A retort formed on Jason's lips, but he refrained. The man had a point.

The paramedics removed two portable oxygen tanks and secured masks on Jason and Melanie.

"Now, let's see those burns." Brent held out Jason's arm and inspected the red marks. "Not too bad. More like a sunburn. Anywhere else?"

Jason reached for his shirttail. Might as well let his friend have a look. "My back took the brunt of the heat." The mask muffled his words.

The paramedic lifted the garment and whistled.

"It doesn't feel *that* bad." Jason glanced over his shoulder.

Brent shook his head. "It's not. I'm amazed at the lack of severity. Your back is red and angry, but like your arms, it looks like a bad sunburn." Brent flipped open his case and retrieved a small tube. He smeared burn cream on Jason's arms and back. "That should help. If you've got any aloe at home, I'd use that if you need relief from the sting."

"Will do." Jason straightened his shirt and held his arms out to the side, allowing the medicine to do its thing.

After having his vitals taken for the third time and spending ten minutes breathing in clean air, Jason removed the plastic cover from his mouth. He stood and scanned the crowd that had gathered at the police-guarded perimeter. Was the creep out there examining his handiwork? He withdrew his phone from his jeans pocket and snapped pictures of the crowd gawking from behind the yellow crime-scene tape.

Sheriff Monroe joined him. "You two okay?"

Jason glanced at Melanie then back to Dennis. "Yeah." He narrowed his gaze. "Dude, what happened to you?"

Monroe brushed his damp pant legs and cringed. "Got a call from Harvey. His truck ran out of gas. I took him some. His dog jumped on me and knocked the gas can out of my hands and all over my jeans."

Jason chuckled. "Well, don't get too close to those flames."

"I hear ya." Dennis crossed his arms over his chest and stared at the burning building.

VSPD officer Lance Olsen strode over. "Cooper. Monroe."

"Olsen," Jason and his boss responded in unison.

Jason tucked his phone in his pocket.

Lance jutted his chin toward the crowd. "I'm thinking the same thing. We're getting pictures, too." The officer produced a small notebook and pen. "Want to tell me what happened?"

Not really. He wanted to get Melanie out of here. But Jason knew the man needed his statement. He proceeded to give a rundown of what happened, and Melanie added a few details when she could. Jason held up his palms. "As you can see, there's not much that will help."

"I'll contact Mrs. Evans. Maybe she noticed something on her walk home." Olsen tapped his pencil on his notebook. "Anything else you can think of?"

"No. I wish… Wait. I did see Laney Wilson stop and talk with Miss Judith before I went back into the apartment. Maybe give her a call. I doubt she'll have anything to add, but you never know."

"Got it." Lance finished his notes then slipped the pad of paper into his pocket. "I'll keep you guys in the loop."

"'preciate that." The sheriff shook Olsen's hand.

Lance clasped Jason's shoulder. "Take care of yourself."

"Will do. And thanks."

Officer Olsen strode off, no doubt to interview those gawking at the fire.

Red and blue lights flashed, casting color across Melanie's face. Her quietness increased Jason's concern. His desire to get her away from the scene grew.

Dennis leaned next to Jason's ear. "Take her home. Get her away from all this. I'll call you later."

Jason nodded and watched as Monroe ducked under the crime-scene tape and disappeared out of sight.

He turned to Melanie and squeezed her arm. "Ready to go?"

She dipped her chin and shrugged. Accepting his outstretched hands, she struggled to her feet.

The hairs on the back of his neck stood. His gaze darted along the perimeter.

Melanie's attacker lingered out there. Watching. He could feel it.

The old Evans place loomed before her. The sights, sounds and smells of her childhood memories rushed back. Almost like if she tried hard enough, she could step out of the truck and into the past. Fingers splayed on the glass of the passenger window, she sucked in a ragged breath. Funny how every detail of her life ran like a vivid movie in her brain. Except for two days. The two days she desperately needed to recall. But no matter how hard she tried, the memories refused to come.

Shoulders slumped, Melanie stared at the updates Jason had made. He'd done an amazing job maintaining the original character of the old house and yard.

The farmhouse had a modern appearance. Jason had

kept the white exterior, but added blue trim to the windows and pine beams to the large porch.

Her gaze landed on the old oak tree in the front yard ringed with multiple varieties of hostas. The clean lines and simple landscape created an indescribable tranquility.

The scene pulled at her numb emotions. She'd come here as a child for shelter from her parents' blatant disregard for her feelings. And now, she returned to the same house for protection from a madman. Her personal refuge. The house had been healing for her once—could it happen again?

The driver's-side door slammed closed, jolting her from her thoughts.

Jason trotted around the truck and opened her door. "Welcome to my home."

She scanned the familiar neighborhood. The idea of Valley Springs as home had never occurred to her. Not after her horrible experiences. But an unexplained warmth filled her chest. Accepting his hand, she continued to gape at his beautiful house as she slid from the seat. When her feet hit the ground, her knees buckled.

"Whoa." Jason's arm circled her waist. "I've got ya."

"Thanks." What else could she say? Her body protested every movement. How much could one person take before they crumbled? Something told her she was about to find out.

"Hang on. Let me grab your bag." He reached behind her.

"My bag?" Her mind scrambled to catch up with his statement.

He pulled her duffel from the back seat and slung it over his shoulder. Hand on her elbow, he escorted her to the black door marking the entrance.

"I'd forgotten you'd taken my things to the truck.

Seems like days ago that you did that." Had it only been four hours?

"Hard to believe we had planned to come over here this afternoon." He released her arm and inserted the key into the lock. "I hope you like what I've done with the place. I wanted to keep true to my childhood memory, but also make it mine."

The door opened, and Melanie stepped inside. Her jaw dropped. A beautiful black leather couch, accented by blue denim and yellow pillows, greeted her. But the wood-slab coffee table took her breath away. She shuffled into the living room and ran her fingers along the natural stone that framed the fireplace.

"It's just like I remember, minus Mrs. Evans's floral decor." She spun in a slow circle. "It's amazing."

"I'm glad you like it."

"Has Mrs. Evans seen what you've done?"

"She has. Wanted to know if I'd sell it back to her." He chuckled.

He secured the lock and pointed her in the direction of the kitchen. "I'll make you a cup of tea to calm those nerves, then take your bag to the guest room." He placed her duffel at the entrance of the hall and followed her into the kitchen. He flipped the burner on under the teakettle and put together a plate of crackers and cheese. After placing the snack on the table, Jason excused himself to take her things to her temporary bedroom.

Melanie thought she'd hidden her nerves, but she hadn't fooled Jason. Although, why had she expected to? He'd always read her moods with a surgeon's precision. She proceeded to nibble on the tasty morsels while waiting on the water to boil.

The high-pitched whistle of the kettle signaled the

water was ready. Jason slipped into the kitchen and busied himself making her tea.

"Why buy a big house? You have plans for a wife and kids?" Her cheeks heated. She had no business asking about his personal life. One that she'd pictured herself a part of as a teenager. A dream that had disintegrated when her stupid brain refused to work. She stuffed a cracker layered with cheese in her mouth before she made a fool of herself.

"Someday, I'd like to have a family. I thought I'd found the right woman once, but it didn't work out."

She jerked her gaze to his. He stared at her for a moment too long. Could he have meant her when they were younger? Doubtful. He'd never shown an interest. Of course, the four-year age difference hadn't been conducive to a romantic relationship. She'd probably read too much into his statement and refused to embarrass herself by asking what he'd meant.

"That's too bad." She bit her lip. What did it matter now? Too much time and too much pain had passed between them. He was her best friend's irritated brother. Nothing more.

He handed her a cup. "So there's no boyfriend out there I should call for you?"

She snorted. "Not likely. I'm not good at relationships. Anyway, thanks for the tea. I think I'll take it to my room." She inhaled the peppermint scent. Her favorite. Had he remembered? She wrapped her fingers around the mug, letting the warmth seep into her hands, and rose from her chair. "And, Jason... I appreciate all you've done."

"Good night, Melanie."

With a forced smile, she ambled to the guest room. Guessing where he'd delivered her bag, she peered into the first room on the right. Her duffel sat next to the queen-size bed, confirming her suspicions. They might never heal the old wounds, but he hadn't forgotten her love for this room. The intricate details of the carved wooden crown molding and the stained-glass windows lining the upper part of the wall warmed her heart.

The room had been Mrs. Evans's favorite. The woman's craft room, where she'd taught Melanie how to cross-stitch all those years ago.

Childhood memories flooded in. Everything except the abduction. Even fifteen years later, the events of those nights eluded Melanie. Only one recollection remained crystal clear. Allison had begged her to go for help. Her friend had suffered at the hands of their captor and had pleaded with Melanie that if the opportunity came, she should leave and find help.

Tears threatened to fall, but Melanie refused to give in to the frustration. Maybe someday she'd remember everything. Her therapist had said it could happen at any time, or her brain might keep it locked away forever. Her mind screamed at her to leave the pain in the past, but her heart insisted she find Allie's killer. And the only way to do that was to remember.

Melanie dug through her bag to retrieve her toiletries and made her way to the bathroom. After showering the grime from her skin and hair, she changed into sweats. Fatigue consumed her and forced her to get some rest. She crawled under the covers and faced the windows. She'd come to Valley Springs for closure and instead found a man who wanted her dead. Why had he targeted her? She only wanted to do her job and search for Allison's body. She should have known life wouldn't be that simple.

Shadows danced behind the curtain-covered glass, igniting her nerve endings. Was her attacker out there, waiting to burn her alive again? She rolled onto her back and pulled the comforter to her chin.

Staring at the ceiling, she chewed the inside of her cheek. *Lord, why is this happening to me?* That was selfish. Jason had risked his life for her. She should focus on him, not herself. *I'm sorry for only thinking of myself, Lord. Shield Jason from danger. I know he still blames me for leaving Allie, but he's put his animosity aside to protect me. Please keep him safe.*

As she tossed and turned, her mind relived each attack, searching for what she'd done to provoke the masked man. Sleep eluded her. She gave up and padded down the hall. Her heart skittered. With each step, the image of her assailant pounced from the dark corners. She wrapped her arms around her waist and continued her trek, her gaze darting to the hidden areas in the hall.

A light glowed beyond the kitchen doorway. Melanie shook off the shiver mounting at the base of her neck and stepped into the dimly lit room.

Jason sat at the table, laptop in front of him, and papers scattered across the surface. A frown marred his handsome face.

Melanie braced her hand on the doorjamb. "Whatcha workin' on?"

He jolted and knocked several documents to the floor. "Would you not do that!"

"Sorry. Didn't mean to." She kneeled to gather the papers and halted. Her own face stared back at her—the photos of her taken after she'd escaped from her captor. Two days' worth of bruises littered her face. Bile rose in her throat, and phantom pains shot through her face and arms. Her mind remembered the agony of her injuries. Why not the details?

"Melanie." Jason's hands gripped hers. "Let me." He slipped the picture from her hand and collected the others, then placed them on the table.

Her teeth chattered. "Why do you have those?"

"I'm a detective." He wrapped his arm around her waist and lifted her to her feet.

"No." She didn't believe him. If that was true, he'd work on the case at the office, not in his kitchen at two in the morning. "What's the real reason?"

He studied her, then sighed. "I've pored over the information for years. I can't stop until I find my sister."

"Jason, she's dead," Melanie croaked. The report had to have more than enough data to come to that conclusion.

His shoulders drooped. "I know that. The evidence is unmistakable. But I have to find Allie's body and put the person responsible behind bars. I owe her that."

"Me, too."

Jason narrowed his gaze. "What do you mean?"

She ran a hand over her face. Great. Now he thought she had confessed to abandoning Allie to fend for herself. "It's not what you're thinking. Contrary to your belief, I didn't save myself and leave Allison to die." How did she make him understand? "She's why I came back to Valley Springs. Why I became a forensic anthropologist. I owe it to Allie to bring her home for a proper burial. And to finally remember what happened during the days we went missing, so the person responsible can pay." The last sentence came out as a whisper.

A cold chill wound up Melanie's back. Her heart pounded. The possibility that her return to Valley Springs had triggered the attacks slammed into her. Had the madman planned to finish what he'd started?

* * *

Her entire life since Allie's disappearance had revolved around finding his sister?

Jason swallowed against the lump in his throat. "Sounds like we have a lot in common." Melanie's puzzled look had a sad smile forming on his lips. "I mean look at us. We both chose careers related to Allie's death."

Her eyes glazed over as if she'd retreated to another world.

"Mel?"

She blinked and straightened her spine. "Yes, we did." She shuffled the photos on the table and studied them one by one.

"Anything useful come to mind?" He cringed. If her memory hadn't returned, his comment made him sound like a jerk. But hadn't he already wrapped up that title in spades? Why he cared if he sounded like a cad after so many years of resentment, he wasn't sure.

"No." She massaged her temples. "The event is still a blank."

Touching his lips with steepled fingers, he studied her. The police report had gaps. The words *no memory* scribbled across those sections spiked his anger. And the places where he expected details were vague statements. He wanted those empty spaces filled in. He'd never wanted to hear her excuses, but something had changed, and he had to know. "You said she had a severe head injury and told you to run, but why would you leave her alone?"

Her mouth gaped open. "Are you ready to listen?"

Was he? If he wanted to solve the case, what choice did he have? "Yes. I want to know what happened." His stomach clenched. He'd secretly hoped Melanie hadn't disappointed him, but in the past, the risk of confirming his suspicions had outweighed his need for the truth. Instead, he'd held it against her and refused to hear her side of the story. Until now.

A chair scraped across the floor, and she lowered herself onto the seat. "I don't recall much. My therapist calls it dissociative amnesia. She said I might never regain my memory of what happened. Even warned me against trying. But I have to remember. I need to remember." Her fingers smoothed the edge of a place mat.

He sat motionless, hoping she'd continue.

She pulled in a deep breath and bit her bottom lip. "Allie's eyes. They haunt me in my sleep. She pleaded with me to go for help if I ever got free. Told me not to help her, but to run." Her unfocused gaze remained on an imaginary spot on the table.

The tick of the clock echoed in his ears. He pinched the bridge of his nose. "Why would Allison do that?"

Tears streamed down her cheeks. Her wide-eyed gaze met his. "Because she'd lost so much blood from a head wound, she knew if I stayed, we'd both die."

The air whooshed from his lungs. He'd seen Melanie's battered body after she'd escaped, but in his mind, Allie hadn't suffered the same torture. He'd been wrong. So wrong. If he was honest with himself, he should have known better. His little sister had suffered, and he'd been powerless to help.

"I—I hadn't realized." He forced his dinner to stay where it belonged.

"You never asked." Fire lit behind her eyes, and Melanie's voice skyrocketed. "You never listened." Her clenched fists trembled.

The muscles in his neck tightened, and an intense ache formed around the crown of his head. He knew deep down where logic resided that Melanie hadn't aban-

doned his sister, but the brother in him wouldn't release
the anger that she'd left his baby sister in the hands of
a maniac. But that was *his* problem. She had enough of
her own.

"I have to know, was she—? Was she dead when you
got out?" His pulse raced.

Her lips pursed, and she looked away. "I don't know."

"How could you not know?" A muscle twitched in
his jaw.

"I can't remember," she whispered. "My stupid brain
won't release the memories." She grabbed handfuls of
her hair and groaned.

Silence descended. The heater hummed, and the wind
kicked up outside, rattling the screens on the kitchen
windows.

Oh, Allison, what happened to you?

"I'd like to help you review the case." Melanie's soft
voice filled the quiet.

Her words infiltrated his thoughts. He cleared the
lump in his throat. "I'm not sure that's a good idea."

"Why not? I'm a professional that works on cold cases
all the time." She folded her arms across her chest.

"I'm not implying that you can't do it—"

"You just don't want me to." Melanie threw the words
in his face.

He ran his fingers through his hair. She had him there.
Was he so determined to force her out of the case that he'd
risk not solving his sister's murder? He'd made a vow to
Allie that he'd do everything in his power to bring her
home. But he never imagined it would include working
with Melanie. Resigned to his decision, he sighed. "All
right. We can work together. Never know, you might remember what happened."

She blanched. "We can always hope."

He gathered the photos, organized them and handed her the stack of images. "Let's try this in a systematic fashion. Start with those. They aren't the easiest to look at, but any insight will help." He'd purposely placed the image of the cabin on top and those of her at the bottom.

Melanie stared at the wooden structure, then flipped to the next picture. Her eyes glazed over.

"Mel?"

Her lack of response had Jason leaning in to get a glimpse of what had sent Melanie into a catatonic state. The room where her kidnapper had held her and beaten her sat before him. Round hooks protruded from the rock wall, and his sister's blood covered the floor. He shut off his inner detective and looked at it from a victim's point of view. For the first time, he saw the evidence from a different perspective. The sensation of terror jumped from the page and clawed at him like a wild animal.

He slipped the photos from her fingers and cupped her cheek. "Don't. It's not worth putting you through the trauma."

Her gaze shifted to him. The pain in her brown eyes made him flinch. She blinked. Life seeped into her, and she drew in a shaky breath.

"That's it. Come on back." Jason considered her physical response. There was more to her story than she'd told him. But what? The wind whooshed from him like he'd been punched in the gut. He dipped his chin and peered up at her. "You have PTSD, don't you?"

She sniffed and nodded.

"Why didn't you tell me?" It hurt she hadn't confided in him. Then again, she had no reason to trust him, the way he'd acted toward her.

"I didn't want your pity."

Oh, Melanie. He had to do something to bridge the gap that had grown between them.

"Can we start over? I know it's my fault, and I can't promise my bitterness won't sneak up on me. But I hate the tension between us. We have to work together if we want to solve this case, and I'm willing to put my anger aside…or at least I'm willing to try."

Her bottom lip quivered. "On one condition."

"What's that?"

"Don't treat me like I'm made of porcelain, and that includes working Allie's case. I'm doing this."

Could he include her without her shattering? But wasn't that her point? To treat her like the strong woman she'd grown into.

"Deal." He fought the urge to pull her into a hug. He might have agreed to work on their fractured relationship, but her part in Allison's death continued to trouble him.

She hugged her waist. "I've missed our friendship."

A sad smile formed on his lips. He had, too, but admitting that to Melanie would absolve her of her actions. And he couldn't do that—not yet. "Let's get to work."

Disappointment flashed across her face, then vanished. "Okay."

He had to tread lightly. Their truce stood on shaky ground, but at least it existed.

An hour later, Jason checked the locks on the doors and confirmed the deputy assigned to monitor his house had arrived and parked out front. He ambled to his room and placed his Glock on the nightstand. His body demanded sleep, but his brain ran like an out-of-control train.

Excitement flowed through his veins. A few pieces of Allie's case had taken shape, thanks to Melanie's determination. In fact, he and Melanie had worked well together. A truth that grated on him. The pictures and case documents had driven him to the brink of snapping at her, but he'd refrained. She'd pushed through agonizing information and hadn't blinked. Whether he wanted to or not, he had to admire her tenacity.

Hours had passed, and he'd forgotten about the pictures on his cell phone. He exhaled and removed the phone from his pocket. Scrolling through the pictures he'd taken at the fire, he studied the faces. No one stood out. Each person an image of fear and sadness. He flipped to the final photo and squinted. What was Uncle Randy doing at the fire scene?

Jason forwarded the pics to Keith and tossed aside his phone. His uncle's presence at the apartment fire baffled him. Why would Randy be there? Maybe he'd come to town for a late dinner. He tucked away the information to mull over later.

After he changed, he dropped into bed and yanked the comforter over him. He needed rest to be on top of his game. Tomorrow held a new set of problems. Melanie wanted to return to work, and that meant she'd be out in the open, vulnerable to another attack. Who was behind these attempts on her life? He'd check with Keith, see if the man had discovered anything from her previous employer. If not, he'd take a closer look at her arrival into town.

It didn't matter how he felt about her, which, to his astonishment, had changed over the past couple of days. He had to figure out who had her in his crosshairs.

Melanie held the key to finding Allie, and her assailant hadn't backed down. Jason refused to give up and had committed, if only to himself, to keep her alive.

FIVE

The warmth from the sun sent rivulets of sweat trickling down Melanie's back. She'd shed her normal coverall attire, worn to exhume remains, hours ago. The exertion had made the outer layer of material like a sauna. Her jeans and new Anderson County Sheriff's Department navy blue T-shirt clung to her like a second skin. The normal cool Indiana winter had delayed its arrival, and here she stood, hot and sticky.

She dusted off her hands on her jeans and breathed a sigh of relief. It had taken her three days to finish the exhumation of the unknown skeleton. Thanks to her attacker, six days had passed since the hikers' discovery.

She'd prepped the boxes and bags that sat in the van, ready for transport.

Deputies had roamed the woods around her work area, and Jason had stood like a sentinel every day. The attack was never far from her mind as she'd collected evidence and documented locations and specific bones. Several times she'd found herself looking over her shoulder, unable to shake the odd sensation of being watched.

The work had left her exhausted but satisfied. Finding the entire skeleton—an unusual feat in her line of work—gave her a jolt of satisfaction. Most digs left her searching for a few missing bones, but not today. Every piece had been accounted for. She'd confirm the dates upon further examination, but she could confidently say the girl had been killed two to five years ago, giving the police a time range to search the missing-persons database. Overall, a successful day.

She slapped the rear doors of the white ACSD lab van. "Go on, Daniel. I'll see you tomorrow."

The tech stuck his head out the driver's side window. "You got it, Dr. Hutton. Later." He waved then cranked the engine.

Gravel crunched under the vehicle's tires as Daniel exited the parking lot.

The county had sent an assistant to help her load the evidence and transport it to the lab. Tomorrow she'd examine the remains, but today she'd go to the station, grab a shower and type up her notes. The soreness in her body had increased over the last few days, but she hadn't stopped working. The Jane Doe deserved a quick recovery. With that part of her job complete, Melanie required downtime tonight. A quick glance at her watch confirmed the time. Four in the afternoon. If she hurried, she'd finish her task and be ready to call it a day no later than five o'clock.

She inhaled. The scent of pine lingered in the air, filling her with a sense of calmness she hadn't experienced since she'd arrived in town. She wanted to stay in the moment, but her long and distinguished to-do list hadn't left much time for relaxation. This discovery, the attacks and her and Jason's personal investigation of Allison's disappearance told her she had to get moving.

Jason's attitude change the other night had thrown her. She'd prayed for years he'd put aside his anger and assumptions, and talk to her. Why his question about starting over had shocked her, she had no clue. She'd asked God, and He had delivered. Jason's request had her heart soaring with possibilities of a solid friendship. As a teen, she'd wanted more, but as an adult and after all that had happened, speaking terms would be a relief.

A twig snapped to her left.

Her heart thundered. She spun toward the edge of the woods, seeking out the cause.

Tree limbs fluttered in the soft breeze. Deputies stood next to their patrol cars waiting for the all-clear to leave. The lack of concern bothered her.

She turned in a small circle. Where had Jason gone?

Dark beady eyes peered at her through the brush.

"Ja-Jason!" she screamed.

He came flying from the trail. "What's wrong?"

"He..." She pointed at the perimeter of the parking lot. "He's out there."

"Get in the truck. Lock the doors. Do not get out until I return." Keys flew in her direction.

She snatched them in midair and hurried to his vehicle. Key fob in hand, her shaky fingers refused to cooperate. *Calm down, girl.* She willed her heart rate to slow. Thumb on the unlock button, the mechanism clicked. She flung open the door and jumped inside. She slammed the door shut and punched the lock. Her breaths came hard and fast. Her limbs went limp, and her pulse raced.

Head back, she closed her eyes. What had she done to deserve being hunted? Was this payback for leaving Allie in the hands of a killer? Or had the killer returned to finish the job he'd started fifteen years ago?

Lord, I've committed my life to a career that allows me to find her body. What else do I need to do to relieve myself from the guilt?

Even as she prayed, she knew better. God had her in

His hands no matter what happened, and she'd do well to remember that.

Knock. Knock.

Melanie shot up straight, her shriek filling the cab. She covered her mouth.

Jason peered in the window. "It's just me, Mel. Open up."

She fumbled for the handle. When the door released, she lurched from the seat and into his arms. She understood the man who held her hadn't completely forgiven her, but right now, she needed her old friend, whether he liked it or not. Her PTSD had snuck in on the edges of her sanity and threatened to take her under, and Jason had become her grounding pole.

What was she going to do? Someone had painted a target on her back, and she was clinging to reality by a thread.

Jason's heart rate jumped at the nearness of the woman in his arms, but his mind demanded he hold on to the pain of the past. The game of tug-of-war between his head and his heart refused to end. He'd carved a tentative friendship with Melanie, but a dark cloud hovered over the fragile agreement.

"We checked out the area. Your masked man is nowhere to be found. I'm guessing he had an escape route planned out." He smoothed his hand down her hair. "Don't worry. We *will* get him. I won't let him hurt you."

She peered up at him. "Jason?"

"Yeah?"

"Could these remains be linked to the person after me?"

Jason had no clue how the old burial site had anything

to do with her. Yet with all the attacks centered around the grave, he'd already considered it.

"I don't know, Mel. I just don't know. But I promise not to ignore the possibility." He tightened his hold and allowed her time to regain control.

Melanie sniffed and straightened. "Sorry I fell apart on you. I, uh—" She brushed his shirt at his shoulder. "I'm not sure why I'm such a mess."

Was she serious? He placed his finger under her chin and lifted. "We may have our differences, but you've impressed me by the way you've dealt with all the craziness over the last week."

Her red puffy eyes widened. "You're impressed with me?"

"Why wouldn't I be?" He tucked a stray hair behind her ear. "I've watched you all day. You do your job with an intensity and professionalism that Valley Springs is fortunate to have. The care you took with the victim was touching. And the attacks haven't slowed you down, even though I know you're hurting."

She brushed more stray hairs from her face. "You're right about one thing. I am sore."

He raised an eyebrow.

She averted her gaze. "And I do each job as if I'm recovering Allison's remains."

Her statement punched him in the gut. Last week, his anger would have controlled his response, but after a couple nights ago, a new perspective had changed his way of thinking.

He cleared his throat. "Someday, I hope you *can* bring Allie home." He motioned for her to climb back in the truck. "I'm sure you want to get out of here and get cleaned up."

"I do. That's the one thing about my job. It doesn't

matter if I wear coveralls or not, I think the dirt is attracted to my hair and skin." She shook her hair, and dirt fell into her lap.

"Then let's go." He closed the passenger door and skirted the truck. He scanned the area one last time before he hopped into the driver's seat and pulled from the parking lot.

With a wave to the patrol officers, he accelerated down the highway toward the station.

He glanced in Melanie's direction. "I talked with Keith while you worked. He said your previous employer agrees with you. The man had no reason to believe the attempts on your life had anything to do with your old cases."

"I know you had to check, but I'm not surprised." She twirled a strand of hair between her fingers. "And before you ask again, I haven't dated anyone since high school."

He gaped at her, then returned his attention to the road. "I'm not even sure what to say to that."

"Nothing to say." She shrugged. "Why would I want to endure the pain of rejection?"

He opened his mouth to question her further, but changed his mind.

They sat in silence for several minutes, his brain spinning with the information.

"If not an old case or an ex-boyfriend, then that leaves a connection to Valley Springs."

She pivoted to face him. "It could have been random."

Now, she was grasping. "I highly doubt that. Once, maybe, but this guy has tried to kill you multiple times. This is not random."

Arms wrapped around her middle, Melanie stared out the windshield. "The question is, why?"

"Don't know. Maybe you interrupted him visiting the grave site the hikers discovered. Or it could be someone with a past grudge." *Like the man who kidnapped you and Allie.*

"I see that look. Don't even go there. Why would our kidnapper target me now?"

He drummed his fingers on the steering wheel. "Maybe he thinks you came back to town because your memories are returning, and he's worried you can identify him."

"But I can't remember. I have no clue who he is." Her voice was so filled with agony it tore him apart.

Jason hadn't wanted to mention the connection to her abduction, but he'd considered that possibility.

"Unit Twelve."

Jason grabbed his radio. "Go ahead, Dispatch."

"Code ten-sixty-five."

"Copy the missing person." His stomach twisted. Living in a small town meant he most likely knew the person who'd disappeared. "Annie?"

"Go ahead, Jason."

"Who?"

"Laney Wilson."

"How long?"

"Her husband said she didn't come home after work last night."

Bile crept up his throat. The woman had two young children and was his good friend's wife. A runaway or an irresponsible individual didn't describe Laney. "Copy that."

Melanie rested her hand on his arm. "Jason?"

He shifted his gaze to Melanie and back to the road. "Laney's twenty-eight. She has a two-year-old and a nine-month-old." They had to find her. Telling Laney's husband—Jason's friend, Tim—anything but good news was unacceptable.

"Lord, please protect this woman. Help us find her alive and safe," Melanie prayed aloud.

How had she kept her faith after the kidnapping and injuries? His own faith had faltered. He still believed, but he couldn't remember the last time he'd prayed after God ignored his pleas for his sister.

With the rest of the crew taking the highway, Jason headed down the county road, taking the back way into town. Deputies would soon be scouring the countryside for any clue to Laney's whereabouts, so he might as well start on his trip home.

Two miles later, Melanie sucked in a breath. "Jason? What's that?"

He slowed and narrowed his gaze on a blue sedan in the ditch. "That's Laney's car."

The vehicle's doors stood open, and the contents of Laney's purse lay scattered on the side of the road.

"I don't like the looks of this." He pulled in front of the sedan and put the truck in Park. "Stay here."

He radioed for backup and slid from his seat. "Be right back."

"Be careful, Jason."

Skirting the car, he peered inside. Drops of blood stained the upholstery. He reached in and pushed the button that popped the trunk. Taking a deep breath, he lifted the lid. Air whooshed from his lungs. No Laney.

Jason stood and scanned his surroundings. He squinted at a truck in the distance. He hadn't remembered seeing it when he arrived at the scene.

The hairs on the back of his neck prickled. Had he missed someone following them?

Gravel crunched behind him. He turned. A tire iron

swung at him. He pulled away but not quickly enough. His head exploded in pain. His body hit the ground, and the world went dark.

SIX

Melanie leaned back against the seat, waiting for Jason to return. She rubbed her temples and cringed. Her bruises had bruises, and the last few days of work had further strained her muscles. She released a long breath.

The radio announcer droned in the background, warning that the first snowfall of the season threatened to hit within the next week. He advised exposure caution with the dropping temperatures and light winds. Mother Nature appeared ready to make up for the mild autumn.

At least Melanie had finished recovering the unknown victim from the shallow grave the hikers had discovered a week ago.

She rubbed her arms to chase away the chill. Spotting a large sweatshirt between the seats, she plunked her cell phone in the cupholder and pulled on the fleece layer. Warmth seeped into her skin, and Jason's lingering cologne teased her senses. He hadn't changed the scent in twenty years. She yearned for the carefree days of their youth. But life had a way of turning the world on its side.

What was taking Jason so long?

Melanie eased from her seat. "Jason? You need some help?" She edged down the side of the truck. "Jason?"

A flash of movement caught her eye. She looked over

her shoulder. A man in a black ski mask blocked her path. She screamed and took off running toward the woods for cover. Where was Jason? Her legs pumped even though they protested at the exertion. The man's footsteps grew closer. If only she could make it to the trees and hide. Jason had called for backup before he'd left to check out Laney's car. More officers would arrive soon. She had to stay alive until help arrived.

Leafless oak limbs drooped, and clusters of evergreens mixed with the setting sun created murky shadows in the woods that loomed ahead. Her chest constricted. She hated the shadows, but right now, the dimness of the copse of trees was her friend.

Her foot hit a piece of wood. A crack sent fear snaking up Melanie's spine seconds before she fell into an opening and hit bottom with a thud. Water splashed around her. Bracing herself on the stone interior, she struggled to her feet. Tremors rattled her body. A foot of freezing cold water covered her boots and the lower part of her legs. Her teeth chattered as she scanned the interior. An old well.

No ladder existed. She examined the crevices between the stones, searching for hand and footholds. Her pulse quickened. Maybe she could climb out. She dug her toes into the gaps and wedged her fingers into the tiny holes and pulled herself upward. Her limbs threatened to give out, but she fought for the next handhold, and the next. The wall crumbled beneath her. She fell, slammed into the other side and plunged into the water at the bottom. Pain shot through her shoulder and hip. Her clothes, now soaked, clung to her body. More cuts and bruises had now been added to her already growing collection. Defeat overcame her, and she slouched against the stone wall. She had no way out. Her attacker would find her, and she'd have no way to escape. Her breaths came quick and shallow. *Well, God, now what?*

Think, Melanie. Her cell phone.

Her hand flew to her back pocket and came up empty. Where had it gone? The events ran through her mind, causing panic to rise in her throat. She'd left it in the truck. She wrapped her arms around her waist and willed her heart rate to slow.

Backlit by the sun, a figure stood at the top of the well and peered in.

"You should have stayed away." The mask over his mouth muffled his words. "But don't worry. I'll be back in a few minutes with my shotgun and finish what I started years ago." He moved from her view.

Time was running out. Would Jason find her, or would the well become her grave?

She screamed for help, praying someone heard her before it was too late.

Dizziness consumed him, and his stomach churned. Gravel crunched beneath Jason as he rolled to his side. He pushed himself up on all fours and groaned. Raising a hand, he touched the back of his skull and cringed at the red liquid covering his fingers.

He blinked, trying to clear the fog. What had happened? Sweat beaded on his forehead even though the temperatures had dropped, and a chill sneaked beneath his jacket.

Swaying, he supported himself against Laney's car to keep from collapsing to the ground. The world gyrated like an uneven spinning top. Whoever had clobbered him had done a good job.

A distant scream pierced the air.

"Melanie?" Jason staggered to his truck. The passenger door hung open. Melanie was gone. "Melanie!" Reaching in, he snagged the radio and updated Dispatch.

He tossed the mic to the floor of the truck and pushed off the door. Stumbling over the ditch, he headed toward the pleas for help.

God, please let me find her in time.

His steps faltered. Had he just prayed? Dried weeds tangled on his feet. He pitched forward but caught himself before he fell.

The voice grew louder. It seemed to be coming from the ground.

"Melanie?"

"Jason! Down here."

He peered into a hole. An old abandoned well...and Melanie was at the bottom of it.

"How? Never mind. Are you okay?" He dropped to his knees.

"Get me out of here before he comes back and kills me."

Jason rose and spun, searching for the person who'd clobbered him and had gone after Melanie.

Sheriff Monroe plodded through the field and joined Jason a minute later. "We got your call. What happened?"

"Got a rope?"

"Sure, in my vehicle. Saw Laney's car. Gonna tell me what's going on?" Monroe stood his ground.

"Get me the rope, and I'll explain everything, but we have to get Melanie out."

As if Dennis realized for the first time that Melanie was at the bottom of the well, the man straightened and took off for his SUV.

Twenty minutes later, Melanie was lying on a stretcher with Ethan and Brent fussing over her. Jason hovered a few feet away, not willing to let her out of his sight. Finding her in that well had shaken him. What if the man returned and made good on his threat?

Dennis draped a blanket over his shoulders and slapped an ice pack in his hand.

He gazed at his boss and lifted the ice pack to his head.

"You have that look. Don't want you going into shock. We'll start the search for Laney. You take care of Melanie. And get that head looked at, would ya?" Monroe patted his back and sauntered off.

"Jason?" The feminine voice had him rushing to Melanie's side.

He clasped her hand. "I'm right here."

"I'm so cold."

"I know, honey. Brent and Ethan will have you warm in no time." He sent a pleading look to his friends, then returned his gaze to her. "What hurts?"

"Shoulder and hip. Landed hard." Her breathy words worried him.

"We'll tell Dr. Jenson."

"No hospital stay," she begged.

Unsure he could keep that promise, he squeezed her hand. "We'll make that call once we get there."

She pulled on his arm. Wide terrified eyes stared at him. "It was him."

"Him who?" He struggled to follow her train of thought.

"The man who kidnapped Allie and me. He's the one trying to kill me. Said he'd finish the job he started years ago." She choked back a sob. Jason inhaled. They now knew the identity of her assailant in an abstract sort of way. It was a start. If he could only figure out who this maniac was, Mel would be safe, and Jason would have the answers he'd searched for since Allie disappeared.

He glanced at Mel.

A shiver snaked up his spine as he walked alongside the gurney. He'd dropped his guard and look what happened. He'd had one job—to protect her—and he'd failed. The events of the last week ran like a film reel in his head. Her attacker continued to get bolder, and Jason had no clue who had her in his crosshairs.

How would he keep her safe?

SEVEN

Melanie's mind wavered in and out of the present. One minute, her attacker stood at the edge of her bed, his teeth glinting in the sunlight. The next, the beeps from the machines and the injuries had her grimacing in pain.

Jason had promised he'd stay close, and she needed him by her side. She hadn't heard his comforting voice in quite a while. At least she hadn't remembered it. Where was he?

A soft whoosh of the door had her eyes fluttering open.

"Well, hello there." A nurse in blue scrubs smiled at her.

Melanie glanced at the woman's name tag. Janie. She knew that name. Searching her mind to figure out from where, it clicked. "It's you again."

Janie chuckled. "I could say the same about you. You deserve a frequent-flyer card." She placed her hand on Melanie's arm. "How ya doing, sweetie?"

"I'm alive, I think." The corners of her mouth curved upward.

"That you are. How's the headache?"

"Still there." She sighed. "Do whatever you need to do. I'm not staying in the hospital."

The nurse pursed her lips, holding back her opinion. "I'll see what I can do."

Melanie's gaze drifted to the door.

Janie checked her vitals. "He's in the waiting room."

She narrowed her gaze. "You read minds now?"

Janie charted her blood pressure and pulse rate, then added pain medication to the IV. "He's pacing like a cat on the prowl, and you can't keep your eyes off the doorway." She shrugged. "Two plus two and all that."

Melanie huffed. "That obvious?"

"Sweetie, I'd have to be blind. So how long have the two of you been together?"

"We haven't—we aren't. Probably never will be." Her heart dropped. In her dreams maybe, but Jason had valid reasons to hold her at a distance.

"Well, then I suggest you figure it out. Love like that doesn't come around every day. Get some rest." Janie tweaked her toe and slipped from the room.

Love? Not a chance. Her childhood crush would remain just that, a crush. Her stupid memory—or lack thereof—had sealed their relationship to whatever you'd call what they had now.

Heart heavy with disappointment, she rested her head on the pillow and let the meds take effect. Her eyelids drooped closed. Her attacker filled her thoughts. Images flashed in her brain, and she struggled to hold on to the moments, but they flitted away.

The truth was beyond her grasp. If her mind cooperated, then maybe this nightmare would end.

"Dude, you're gonna wear a hole in the floor."

Jason held an ice pack to the back of his head and glared at his partner. He didn't need Keith's sass right now.

"She's fine. Doc even said so." Keith sat, legs stretched out, ankles crossed, flipping the pages of his magazine.

Jason had studied every calming landscape picture dotting the taupe-colored walls of the waiting room, but peace eluded him. The mental picture of Melanie at the bottom of the well had seared into his brain, and made his stomach churn.

He was grateful Sheriff Monroe had taken over the search for Laney. He could focus on Melanie and her safety. Something he'd failed to do time and time again.

"Why haven't they let me in to see her?" His imagination ran wild with all the horrible possibilities. When he'd left her in the hands of Dr. Jenson, the man had assured him Melanie wouldn't have lasting effects from her injuries. Jason peeked at the doorway of the waiting room and huffed out his aggravation. Pivoting, he eyed Keith.

His partner rolled his eyes. "Would you sit? You're driving me nuts."

"Fine." He stomped over, dropped into a blue plastic chair and crossed his ankle over his knee. After tossing the ice pack on the side table, he opened a magazine and slammed it shut. Blowing out a quick breath, he jumped up and continued to pace. His head pounded in time with his heartbeat. The doc had looked him over when they'd arrived at the hospital, declared he had a mild concussion and ordered him to take it easy.

Keith snorted. "Man, you have it bad."

"What are you talking about?" He'd never wanted to hit his partner, but the man was pushing him to the limit.

Keith stood and planted himself in front of Jason. "You can deny it all you want, but I've never seen you lose your mind over a woman."

He ran a hand over his hair. Keith had a point; Jason had never cared this much about anyone.

Hand on Jason's chest, Keith narrowed his gaze. "Look, I know you have a lot of past to work through, but for your sake and hers, let it go."

"I'm trying, okay?" He pushed the man's arm away and walked to the window. He stared out into the darkness. The fluorescent lights buzzing above grated on his nerves. He had turned the corner from hostility to a fragile friendship with Melanie. Had he been too late to rediscover the closeness they'd once had? Did he want more?

"Detective Cooper." Dr. Jenson stood at the entrance of the waiting room, stethoscope around his neck and hands in the pockets of his white lab coat. The older man looked as exhausted as Jason felt.

Jason rushed over. "How is she?"

The doctor quirked an eyebrow. "She's fine, like I said before. No broken bones, only bruises. She'll be sore and tired."

He thought his legs might buckle beneath him. "Thanks, Doc. Can I—we—see her now?"

Dr. Jenson pursed his lips, no doubt to hide a smile. "We gave her something for the pain. She should sleep a while. But you can head on back to room two eleven. And relieve the security guard while you're at it."

"Thanks, will do." Jason shook the man's hand and hurried down the hall, not waiting for his partner.

At room 211, he thanked the man standing watch and relieved him of his duty. Hand on Melanie's door, he paused. Once the danger had passed, he'd take a moment and sort through his feelings for Melanie. Until then, he refused to spend his energy on anything but her safety. No matter what Keith had implied. Or his heart told him.

His partner caught up with him and held the door open. "Go on. You know you're dying to."

Jason stepped inside. His gaze lingered on Melanie's pale face. "She looks dead."

His partner smacked him on the back and hissed, "Don't let her hear you say that."

"I meant—" He lowered his voice as not to disturb her.

"I know what you meant. She's tough. She'll rally and be on your nerves again in no time."

He forced a smile. "I hope so." He slipped into the chair next to her bed, then leaned forward and studied her.

Dark circles gave her eyes a sunken appearance. Bruises dotted her cheeks and jawline, and a purple splotch on her collarbone peeked out from under her hospital gown.

His heart ached. There had only been one other time she'd looked worse. Fifteen years ago, the day she'd escaped, and he'd turned his back on her. Due to her injuries, he hadn't been able to see her for twenty-four hours after she'd arrived at the ER. The wait had lit a fire behind his anger. When he'd received the go-ahead to visit her, he walked into her hospital room and demanded she explain herself. The hopeful expression on her face had fallen, and she'd turned from him and never looked in his direction again. He'd stomped out of the room, eliminating a friendship he'd once hoped would become more. True, losing his sister had devastated him, and Melanie's actions had confused him. But his accusations had severed any possibility of reconciliation. If he'd only listened, he might've had the woman of his dreams by his side all these years. Instead, he'd let his anger simmer. Anger that refused to go away.

He rested his chin on his steepled fingers. *Lord, please help her heal.* He froze. His second prayer in less than a day, and he'd once again focused on the woman who had been the source of his fury over the years. He buried his face in his hands. He had a choice. Allow their friendship to flourish or hold on to the thread of bitterness that only bred hatred. But he couldn't seem to clip the strand tethering him to his anger.

The next morning, Keith eased into Melanie's room and handed Jason a cup of coffee. "How's she doing?"

"She's stirred a few times but hasn't woken up yet." Jason let the steam from the cup warm his face.

"That's probably a good thing. She's had it rough lately." Keith sipped his drink.

Jason's phone vibrated in his pocket. He removed it and stared at the screen. His uncle. "Hold on, Uncle Randy," he whispered and left the room. "Okay, go ahead."

"I'm worried about your father."

"What's wrong now?" His shoulders sagged.

"I think you getting hurt last night was too much for him. He's drinking again."

The news of his injuries had traveled fast. Jason sighed. "Where is he?"

"At his place. I went over to help him with some repairs, but he's refusing to talk to me. Just stood there staring at his rose garden with a bottle in his hand."

His uncle sounded worried, but Jason had no idea why. Sounded normal to him. Except for his dad drinking at home and not at the bar. He raked a hand through his hair. Thoughts of Melanie had him torn. Go help his dad or stay and be here when she woke up, like he'd promised.

"What's wrong?" Randy's impatience crept over the line.

"I'm at the hospital. I haven't gotten to talk with Melanie yet."

Silence.

His uncle probably considered him a horrible son for debating between the two. He pinched the bridge of his nose. "All right. I'll go check on him."

"Good. Ben's not acting like himself. Thanks, Jason."

"Sure. I'll leave in a minute." He hung up and placed his hand on the wall. Why had his dad chosen now to have a problem?

Keith stepped into the hallway, and Jason motioned his partner to join him.

"What's up?"

"My dad. I have to go." He glanced in Melanie's direction.

Keith gripped his shoulder. "I've got this. Take care of good ol' dad, and I'll keep your girl safe."

"She's not my girl."

"Yeah, whatever." His partner held up his other hand, stopping Jason's response. "Go. I'll let her know you were here."

He nodded. "Thanks, partner." Jason rushed from the hospital before he changed his mind.

The cold slapped him as he stepped from the building. White wisps swirled from his mouth. Temperatures had dropped even lower this morning. Ducking his chin, he huddled into his jacket and strode across the street to the parking lot. What if he hadn't found Melanie before her attacker had returned to kill her…? No, he wouldn't go there. She was alive, and he'd be thankful for that.

Spotting his vehicle, he used his key fob and hit the remote start. His truck revved to life. A light dusting of frost covered his windshield. With his gloved hand, he swiped the glass. A layer of thin white powder tumbled to the ground. He smacked his hands together, releasing the flakes that clung to the leather. Opening the door, he slipped inside and cranked up the heat. With one last look at the window of Melanie's room on the second floor, he pulled away from the hospital.

At seven in the morning, the roads had a peacefulness about them. No hustle and bustle of people going to work. Dew crystals on the trees sparkled in the rising sun. Soon snow would fall, and Valley Springs would turn into a winter paradise. Unlike his life, which had a dark cloud of uncertainty hanging over it. He was torn between the woman his traitorous heart had come to care about more and more each day and his father, who had lost his way and needed his help.

Now that Jason thought about it, what was his dad doing drinking at this time of morning? Concern wormed its way in. He pushed the accelerator and lurched forward, terrified of what he might find.

He whipped into his dad's driveway and slammed the truck into Park. He swung open his door and had one foot on the ground when he spotted his father.

The man's face tilted toward the sky as he leaned on the decorative wooden fence that stood in front of the huge rose garden. The bottle in his hand confirmed Uncle Randy's concerns.

Jason ambled toward him. He flipped his collar and hunched his shoulders.

The roses had died, and the bushes had turned brown, waiting for spring to arrive so they could bloom once again.

It dawned on him that the garden had come after Allison's death. For years, his mind had focused on his father's state of inebriation, and his brain hadn't processed that fact until now. It made sense. Allie's favorite flower had been roses. Pink, to be specific. And Dad had planted lots of pink roses mixed in with other colors.

"Hey, Dad." Jason rested his boot on the lower rung of the fence.

Ben Cooper gave him a sideways glance. "Son. What are you doing here?"

He nodded to the bottle. *What do you think, Dad?*

"Your uncle called, didn't he?" His father's jaw twitched.

"He was worried about you. Said you refused to speak with him."

"He can mind his own business."

Jason turned his gaze on his dad. Were those dried tears? "What's going on?"

"Nothing. As you can see, I'm not drunk."

"If you keep it up, you will be by noon."

His father scowled and poured the contents of his bottle onto the ground. "Happy?"

"I'd be happier if you'd tell me what's with you and Uncle Randy. You two have always been close."

His dad snorted. "Sure we have."

Either he'd missed something, or the lack of sleep had messed with his brain. He shoved his hands into the pockets of his jacket and shivered. Maybe he could talk his dad into going inside before he left. He glanced at his father's rigid stance—fat chance.

"Since you apparently don't need me, I'll get back to Melanie." He dropped his foot from the fence.

"Is she doing okay?"

Jason stopped and stared at his dad. A deep concern lingered in his father's eyes. "You really do care."

His dad shrugged.

Why had he shown interest, then played it off? Jason tucked away the observation and answered the question.

"She'll be sore, but she's a fighter. I expect her to bug me about getting back to work soon."

His father's hand rested on his shoulder. "Take care of her, son."

Jason nodded and strode to his truck, more confused than ever.

The phone in his pocket buzzed. He yanked out the device. Keith's name appeared on the screen. His pulse raced, and sweat dotted his forehead. "What happened to Melanie?"

"Slow down, man." His partner huffed. "You're lady's fine. In fact, she's driving the doctor nuts about leaving."

"Do *not* let her out of your sight." Jason hopped into his truck and put his phone on Speaker. "I'm on my way."

"I told you. Cool your jets. I'm calling because they found Laney Wilson."

"Is she okay?" His partner's tone gave Jason the answer he needed, but he had to ask.

"No. The scent dogs found her about an hour ago in a secluded section of the old Henry place, not far from where you found her car. She's buried in a shallow grave."

"Then how do they know it's her?" Gravel spit from his truck as he whipped onto the narrow two-lane road and sped toward the hospital. His heart hammered against his breastbone.

"Besides the dogs hitting on her scent?"

There was that. "Yeah, okay. I get it."

"We still need to exhume her body. The dogs could be wrong, but I doubt it. It'll require confirmation, but it seems like a formality. The sheriff wants this done right."

"In other words, Melanie has another grave to dig up." The woman required rest and a few days to recover, but the chances were slim. He wanted that for her, but reality demanded her expertise.

"Yup. Hold on." Keith muted his end, then came back on. "Sorry. Thought I saw your uncle, but it must not have been him."

"Why would Uncle Randy be at the hospital at this time of morning?" One hand on the wheel, Jason rubbed the back of his neck with the other. "Ever get that weird feeling we're missing something?"

"Explain."

"I don't know. Something's going on between my dad and Randy, and neither one is sharing." He scratched his chin. "Back to Laney and Mel. I'm making a small leap here, but my guess is that once the evidence is in, we'll find a connection between the two women. Whoever this killer is, he has a familiarity to this town."

"How about we see if things make sense after we get some shut-eye. I can barely think straight." Keith's heavy tone conveyed his exhaustion.

"I hear ya." Sleep deprivation had sunk in its claws. His ability to keep Melanie safe had dwindled. He needed help. "Hey, Keith?"

"Yeah?"

"Stay at my house. I can't protect Melanie by myself."

"Thought you'd never ask."

Jason's shoulders relaxed. Having an extra set of eyes and ears eased his tension. "See ya in a few."

Fatigue had consumed him, and with a maniac on the loose, he'd never forgive himself if his inability to function caused her more pain.

Allie had been his responsibility, and he'd failed as a brother. He knew the self-blame was irrational, but he couldn't seem to let it go.

If he failed Melanie, he had no idea how he'd dig out from under all the guilt.

* * *

An hour had passed since Melanie had roused from her drug-induced sleep, and still no Jason. He'd promised to be here. The rejection hit hard. He'd walked away fifteen years ago, so why had she thought things had changed?

"Stop that." Keith stood in the doorway with his arms crossed.

She scrunched her brow. "What?"

"You know what. That someone-hurt-my-puppy look." He blew out a breath. "Jason's on his way. He had something he had to take care of."

Tears stung her eyes. She shifted her gaze to the window, away from Keith's scrutinizing stare. "Got it."

"I don't think you do."

She whipped her head around and faced him. "What's that supposed to mean?"

He pursed his lips, appearing to struggle with what to say. "He was a wreck waiting to see you. The man paced like a caged animal." Keith scratched his jaw. "He cares about you…a lot."

She gaped at him. "How do you know that?"

"Come on, Melanie. I can see it every time he looks at you." Keith exhaled and ran a hand through his hair. "Just don't give up on him. Okay?"

She nodded. The news eased her doubt, but until Jason confessed his feelings, she told herself to be cautious. Living through another abandonment from someone she cherished… She'd never recover.

"I—"

Jason burst in the door. His hair shot out in multiple directions, most likely from the stocking cap he held in his hand. His gaze found hers. "I'm so sorry. I was called away."

"It's fine. Keith said you'd be back as soon as possible." She picked at the blanket lying across her.

"I'm going to go hunt down some food." With that, Keith ducked out of the room.

Silence hung in the air as Jason made his way to her bedside.

He cupped her cheek. "I know that look."

His touch sent butterflies fluttering in her stomach. Her brown eyes met his green. "What look?" Her voice shook.

"The one where you don't think you deserve to be treasured." He leaned in, his face mere inches from hers. His breath fanned her cheeks.

She swallowed. The man knew her well even after years apart.

His gaze dropped to her lips and drifted back to her eyes.

Time stood still. Was he asking permission to kiss her?

The door whooshed open, and Jason stepped back.

"I came to…" Nurse Janie bustled in. Her gaze darted between them. "Oops. Sorry about that. I can come back." She turned to leave.

"No, come on in." Jason lowered himself into the chair.

"You sure?" Janie sent a questioning look to Melanie.

Disappointment filled her. Maybe it had been her imagination, and Jason hadn't wanted to kiss her after all. "Positive."

"All right then." Janie rounded the bed and checked Melanie's vitals. "Doc said you can go home as soon as you eat breakfast, and he stops by to give you the stamp of approval."

"Sounds good." But where would she go? Back to Jason's house? Or had he changed his mind about that?

Janie pivoted. Hands on her hips, she glared at Jason. "And you, son, better take care of this young lady. I'm tired of seeing her hurt."

"That's the plan." A look of guilt flashed across his face and vanished just as quickly.

"Glad to hear it." The nurse turned to Melanie and softened her voice. "Detective Young is outside with food. I'll let him in on my way out."

Did Melanie know a Detective Young?

Keith waltzed in with a smirk on his face. "I brought extra since the chow-hound over there will steal half of your meal."

"Ha, ha. Very funny, partner." Jason rolled his eyes.

So, Keith's last name was Young. She almost chuckled out loud for not putting the information together.

Keith placed the tray on the roller table. "I'll go stand guard so you can eat in peace."

It hit her again. The reminder of danger latched on and refused to let go.

Her attention flitted to the window. Was her attacker out there, waiting for her, ready to pounce at any moment?

EIGHT

Soft snores drifted from the master bedroom and the living room. Melanie tiptoed toward the kitchen. She'd have to thank Sheriff Monroe later for assigning a deputy to watch the house for a few hours, allowing Jason and Keith to get some much-needed rest. She'd slept at the hospital, but since arriving at Jason's midmorning, the nightmares of being chased and her time in the well refused to leave her alone. She rubbed her arms to chase away the imaginary chill and continued her trek.

A tired smile formed on her lips. Jason had set the timer on the coffeepot for noon before he'd fallen asleep, and the aroma of fresh brew greeted her. She poured a mug and lowered her battered body onto a chair. Inhaling the bold liquid, the cobwebs scattered from her brain.

Keith had informed her that the search dogs found Laney's body in the early hours before sunrise, and patrol had secured the scene. True, they had to confirm the identity, but deep in her gut, Melanie knew. Those poor little kids had lost their momma. Who would do such a thing? She lifted the cup to her chin. The steam from her drink rose and warmed her face. There was only One who could bring peace to Laney's family.

God, I don't know why Laney died, but please comfort

her husband and children. Help Jason and Keith put the man responsible behind bars.

She wrapped her fingers around her mug and stood. The window beckoned her. She sipped her drink and stared into the backyard—a backyard that held wonderful memories of her childhood. Years before she'd fled to her aunt Heather's, Mrs. Evans had rescued her from a household filled with fake love and false reputations. Melanie's parents had only cared about appearances. She'd come to the Evanses' or hung out with Allie to escape the loneliness of her existence.

The bare trees swayed in the breeze. A squirrel scampered along the fence line, pausing to chatter at the birds, then launched himself onto a limb that bobbed up and down until he scurried up the tree.

"Why aren't you tucked away for the winter, little guy?" she whispered.

"Talking to the wildlife now?"

She jostled her coffee mug.

"Didn't mean to startle you. Thought you heard me come in." Jason poured a cup of java and sauntered next to her.

The warmth of his shoulder against hers sent a shiver up her spine. Her mind tumbled to their almost kiss. She lifted her cup to hide the heat rising in her cheeks.

"Want to check out the treehouse sometime? It's pretty much like we left it. I had to replace a few boards here and there, but otherwise, it's still the same."

Her mind whirled. "Why'd you keep it?"

He brought the cup to his lips, hesitated then took a sip. "You and Allie loved it. I had to repair it."

A golf-ball-size lump stuck in her throat. "You did it because of us?"

He shrugged. "I hate to ask, but are you ready to ex-hume Laney's body?"

His nonanswer didn't escape her. She longed for him to let her into his world. Guess not. Her shoulders drooped. "Not really, but it has to be done." She went over to the sink and set down her mug. "Give me twenty minutes, and I'll be ready to go."

Jason walked over and rested his hand on her wrist. "I didn't mean right now."

"I know, but her husband needs answers."

"Please don't overdo it. This isn't a sprint." His concern melted her heart.

Oh, how she wished his words held the truth. "Isn't it?" She peered into his green eyes. "Laney is dead, and someone's after me. There's a small possibility the two things might not be connected, but with everything we know, I say they are. So I disagree with your premise. This is a race to the finish if I want to stay alive." Her emotions bubbled to the surface. Not wanting him to see her tears, she spun and rushed from the room, leaving Jason standing there, mouth open.

After dressing, Melanie gazed at her reflection in the mirror. Black and purple splotches covered her face, and angry red lines marred her skin. She knew when she'd chosen to come to Valley Springs, her time wouldn't be pleasant, but she'd never anticipated being hunted. Her gaze dropped to her cosmetic case—no use putting on makeup. Her injuries were too extensive to hide. Besides, the only man she wanted to impress had already seen her at her worst.

She gingerly pulled on her shoes and moved to the living room.

Jason and Keith stood huddled, deep in conversation. About her, no doubt.

Standing in the entryway, she added a little extra zip in her voice. "Okay, guys. I'm ready to go."

Keith glanced up and nodded. "I'll go first." He slipped out the front door, gun in hand.

Jason slid his Glock from his holster. "Stay right beside me." He moved next to her, put his arm around her waist and drew her in tight.

A shudder rippled through her; the man wasn't messing around. They stepped outside.

Keith scanned the area and opened the passenger door.

Jason hustled her to the truck.

She hoisted herself onto the seat. "What's the plan?"

Jason directed his comment to Keith. "I'll head out. You follow. Keep your eyes open."

"Got it." Keith hurried to his car and jumped in.

Jason's green eyes met her brown. "Ready?"

Was she? She'd be out in the open, vulnerable to the man who'd attacked and threatened her. But she didn't have a choice—Laney needed justice. She nodded.

He latched her door closed and trotted to the driver's side. He reached over and covered her hand with his. "I promise I won't leave you alone." His eyes begged her to believe him.

"I know you won't." She squeezed his fingers. He hadn't said anything, but she knew guilt had eaten at him for not protecting her last time—an all-too-familiar feeling.

Heart pounding in her chest, she took deep breaths to keep the panic attack at bay. Now wasn't the time for a full-blown meltdown. She had a job to do and people counting on her. She had to preserve the evidence so her report would hold up in court when they found the man responsible. Years ago, she'd vowed not to let someone suffer if she could prevent it. Another promise she'd made to herself as a result of the actions of her past.

The tires hummed, and trees whizzed by. Alone in her thoughts, Allie's image entered her mind. Her friend's hands cuffed to the stone wall and her bruised face. The memory of the agony in Allison's voice punched her in the gut, stealing her breath.

Allie, what happened during those two days?

If her brain cooperated, they'd find the man who'd killed Allison, and maybe, just maybe, he'd tell them where he buried her body. But, as of this moment, the events stayed locked away.

The truck bounced on the uneven dirt road, jolting her to the present. The potholes jarred her throbbing hip and shoulder. She bit her lip to keep from crying out.

"Almost there." Jason pointed to the row of vehicles next to the shallow ditch alongside the lane.

"Time to get to work." She inhaled and waited for him to park, then slid from his truck. Her legs wobbled. She grabbed the doorframe and prayed her body held out long enough to recover Laney and get the woman to her family as quickly as possible. She released the truck and closed the door. Each step had her grimacing. Everything hurt, but she'd withhold that information from Jason. He had enough on his mind with keeping her safe.

Jason placed a warm hand on the small of her back as he led her to the scene. His gaze rotated from one side to the other, in a constant scan of the area. "I gave Kyle, another ACSD detective, a call and asked him to drop off your equipment. Everything will be waiting for you."

"Thanks." Her muscles tensed. His actions only reminded her of the seriousness of the situation.

An hour later, Melanie bent to retrieve her hand trowel and grimaced. The laborious work had highlighted every ache and pain sustained over the past week. For the first time since she'd become a forensic anthropologist, she wanted a long vacation. But she had a mission and vowed to push forward until she completed her goal—finding Allie's remains.

Laney's body lay before her on a bed of dirt. The county medical examiner hovered nearby. If the body hadn't required an autopsy, as county coroner, Melanie could have handled the crime scene herself.

The man's impatience grated on her nerves, but she had no intention of missing a single piece of evidence, so he needed to chill out.

Melanie peered up at the ME. "You can stop looking at me like that. It's not going to make me move any faster."

The man harrumphed. "The last forensic anthropologist we contracted didn't take forever." He folded his arms across his chest. "And, by the way, who'd you bribe to get on the payroll?"

She'd mentally asked that question multiple times. Who had funded her position? The bigger question— would she stay after completing her mission of finding Allie's body? Watch Jason move on with his life, have a wife and family? No. Bearing that kind of pain would be impossible.

Ignoring the ME's barb, she snapped several pictures, made notes on her chart and continued the painstaking process of extracting the young mother's body.

Her stomach churned. Bones were normal, even decomposing skin, but the sight of a death twenty-four hours after the person's last breath… She shook her head to dislodge the searing memory. Something she'd have to get used to with her new part-time appointment as coroner.

"Looks like you're almost ready for Greg." Jason stooped at the perimeter.

She sat on her haunches. "Who?"

"The ME, Dr. Vogel." He jabbed his thumb toward the guy leaning against a tree.

"Oh, you mean Dr. Doom over there?"

Jason coughed to cover his laugh. "Never heard him called that before."

"What can I say. He's glaring at me like I'm making him wait on purpose." She brushed a wisp of hair from her forehead with the back of her wrist. "She'll be ready to transport soon." Melanie pointed to the blue tarp, and he handed it to her. "Thanks."

"Don't worry about Greg. He's good at what he does." Jason glanced at Vogel and grinned. "I have a feeling he's not used to waiting. Normally we're the ones waiting on him."

She nodded and focused on her work. The ME would just have to be patient. She had to do this right in the event the case ever went to court. "Guess he'll learn something new today," she grumbled.

Jason snorted. "Are you always so sarcastic?"

"Nah, I'm just out of sorts." She bit her bottom lip. She'd forgotten these people weren't used to working with her yet. "It's kind of a bad habit when I'm waist-deep in a burial site. Sorry."

"No need to apologize. I think it's kinda cute."

Cute? She squinted, considering him. His mischievous smile reminded her of the young boy she used to know. Butterflies took flight in her stomach. If only she could admit her feelings to him without the fear of rejection.

Get back to work and quit dreaming about what you can't have.

Later that afternoon, after she supervised Laney's extraction and the woman's body was lying inside the black bag, the ME placed his fingers on the zipper. The man vibrated with impatience to leave.

"Hold up." Melanie squinted at the deceased. She grabbed her camera and moved around the body, snapping multiple photos.

Dr. Vogel rose and shoved his fists on his hips. "I thought you were done."

Jason arched an eyebrow, and a small smile escaped.

She ignored Jason's amused expression and clicked a few extra pictures for safety's sake.

"Okay. Now you can zip it up."

Dr. Vogel grunted and prepared the bag for transport.

"Make sure you send me the results from the bruises on her neck." Acid burned in Melanie's stomach. Her suspicions ate away at her professional demeanor.

The ME's eyebrows rose to his hairline.

"Please." She forced a smile.

He waved at her like swatting a fly. "You'll get them."

"Wanna tell me what that was about?" Jason folded his arms over his chest.

Melanie held the camera away from herself and offered the preview screen. "See the bruising on her neck?"

He nodded.

"I'm thinking strangulation."

He examined the image and scowled.

She shifted the photo back to her line of sight. "The bruising isn't conclusive yet, but I suspect when Dr. Vogel looks closer, he'll find finger markings on her skin. That's why I want the details from the ME."

"That's personal." He eyed her with concern.

Jason had a point. Melanie swallowed the bile creeping up her throat. "Was he out here burying her body when we arrived?"

He studied Melanie a moment. This could have been her.

"He threatened me. He told me he'd finish what he'd started years ago." Dots danced along the edge of her vision. Melanie inhaled, willing herself to remain in the moment and not tumble back in time.

Jason grabbed the camera and stared at the image of Laney's throat. Melanie shut off the viewer, not wanting the reminder that the maniac had killed Laney and had threatened her. "Let's get back to work."

"Mel."

"No, Jason. I can't discuss it right now." She returned to the crime scene and transferred the evidence to large tubs, then folded the tarps.

Jason joined her. Neither said a word while they placed the equipment in his truck and traipsed back to the site for a final load.

"I'm done here. We can release the scene." She picked up the box of collected evidence and followed her personal bodyguard to his vehicle. She slid the container in the back and hoisted herself onto the passenger's seat. "All seemed quiet out there today."

He pulled away from the site. "We had your back, but don't let your guard down."

"As if." She'd been in the zone while working the exhumation, but since she'd finished, her nerves had tightened like guitar strings. She shifted to look at him and froze. The man had a death grip on the steering wheel.

Jaw set, his concentration darted between the road and the rearview mirror.

"Jason?" She twisted to look out the back window between the headrests. A back spasm had her gritting her teeth. She eased herself to face forward and collapsed back against the seat.

"Thought we had someone following us." He pushed a couple of buttons on his cell phone.

"What's up?" Keith's chipper tone filled the cab.

"Possible tail."

"On it." Two words from Jason, and Keith went from fun to serious in an instant.

"I'm heading home, but we'll take the scenic route."

"Copy that. See you there." Keith ended the call.

"It's probably nothing, but we can't be too careful." Jason sat straighter and stopped talking, his attention solely on his surroundings.

Melanie double-checked her seat belt and stared at the side mirror.

When had her life come to this? The city sounded better all the time, but she'd made a promise to herself and Allison. She'd find her friend's remains and bring Allie home no matter what.

And that *what* just might kill her.

"Whatcha workin' on?" Jason slipped in beside Melanie at the kitchen table.

Jason had determined the tail had been a false alarm, and they'd arrived home several hours ago. After a quick nap, Melanie had Daniel drop off a case file, then absconded to the kitchen and hadn't come up for air or coffee since.

"Looking at my notes for the exhumation at the trail. I've narrowed down the age of the bones. You'll be able to target your search to two to three years ago." She stretched her arms above her head and lowered them, but not before he saw pain flash across her face.

The woman had worked long and hard today and

needed rest. He'd pleaded with her, but she'd refused to quit. He hadn't blamed her. There were three cases that needed their attention. Technically two, since they now knew that the attacks on Melanie and Allie's case were connected. Even though he and Keith could be brought in to investigate Laney's murder at any time, the sheriff had assigned Kyle Howard as lead detective, giving Jason the opportunity to focus on Melanie. Her safety was a high priority for all of them. However, he knew Melanie had a stake in the young mother's case and planned to help in any way possible.

"That will help a lot, thanks." He jutted his chin toward the report. "Would you like a fresh set of eyes?"

"Sure." She handed him the document.

"What am I looking at?" He perused the page.

Her brow furrowed, and she bit her lip. Leaning in, she tapped her fingernail on the third paragraph. "Check out the item found at the Myers Lake Park scene."

"A necklace."

"Go ahead." She nodded.

What was she getting at? He narrowed his gaze. Nothing else in the notes grabbed his attention. The answer had to be in the images. "Have a close-up of the jewelry?" Several matte photographs landed in front of him. After examining each one, he gave her a puzzled look. "The chain's broken."

"Indeed." She tapped on the picture she'd taken at the burial site the hikers had discovered. "The girl must have been wearing it when her killer buried her. And look at the shape. Two interlocking circles, one small, one big. Like those mother-daughter necklaces."

He scratched the stubble on his jaw and studied her expression. "You think this was an abduction gone wrong?"

"I'm leaning that way. But it's only a theory. I need to examine the bones."

"Do you think you can get DNA?"

"It's possible for identifying the victim, but as for the person responsible…don't hold your breath. But, I'll see what I can do once I get to the lab. Never know. If the person responsible touched that chain in any way, like if he strangled the girl, we might find traces of DNA."

He pushed from the table and sauntered to the refrigerator. He pulled out a pitcher of lemonade, poured two glasses and handed one to Melanie. Glass to his lips, he stared at the closed blinds on the window and pondered the information. "What about Laney? You really think it's your kidnapper?"

Melanie took a sip then scrunched her forehead. "The fact she was around at the time of the fire gives me pause." Her hands shook as she placed the glass on the table.

The memories couldn't be easy. They weren't for him. Jason gave her credit; she was holding it together, if only by a thread.

"Why kill Laney?" Melanie whispered.

He'd considered that question for hours. And only one thing made sense. "She had to have seen who started the fire. Or at least the guy thought she did." He'd seen Laney drive past Melanie's apartment that night. That had to be the link.

"It's my fault she's dead. If I'd stayed away…" Her voice trailed off.

The wood floor in the living room creaked.

Melanie's hand flew to her throat.

Finger to his lips, Jason slid his weapon from his holster. Keith had sacked out in the other extra bedroom so he'd be rested to stand watch tonight. The chances of it being him were thin.

After Laney's disappearance, Melanie falling into the well and the discovery of Laney's murder, he planned to have himself or Keith on constant guard duty until he found the creep. Apparently, his instincts had been right.

With Melanie tucked behind him, he moved silently to the doorway. Glock pointed down, he snuck into the living room.

Jason aimed his gun at a figure standing in the entry. "Freeze. Police."

"Jason? It's me, Uncle Randy."

He flipped on the lights. Randy stood with his hands in the air. Keith, with rumpled clothes and bed-mussed hair, had joined him and was holding his weapon on Jason's uncle.

"What are you doing here?" Was the man crazy entering his house unannounced? Randy had to know Jason would be on high alert.

Jason holstered his Glock.

Keith followed suit, tucking his gun inside the back of his waistband. His partner stood with feet apart, arms crossed.

Uncle Randy's arms lowered. "Heard about Laney and came to check on you. I know you and her husband, Tim, are good friends."

"Haven't had much time to process it." Jason glanced behind the man at the front door, then back to his uncle. "How'd you get in?"

Randy brushed his hand over the top of his hair and blew out a breath. "Saw your truck. Knocked. When no one answered, I tried the door. It was unlocked, so I let myself in to see if everything was okay."

Keith shot Jason an are-you-serious look.

Randy's story sounded reasonable, but Jason had secured the front door. He knew he had. No cop worth anything would be that careless.

Melanie stepped beside him. Tension rolled off her like clouds in the middle of a thunderstorm. "Hello, Randy."

His gaze shifted to Melanie. Her white-knuckle grip on the doorjamb puzzled him, but he couldn't blame her. She'd suffered multiple times at the hands of a madman. Her nerves had to be shot. He returned his attention to his uncle. "We were in the kitchen. Must not have heard you."

"Don't worry yourself. Glad to see everyone's okay. I'll head on out." Randy pivoted and strode to the door. "Take care, you three. See ya later."

With that, his uncle left them standing in stunned silence.

"Does he have a key?" Keith demanded.

"Not that I know of. My dad doesn't even have one." He loved his family, but with his father's drinking, he hadn't trusted the man in a long time.

"Then how did he get in? 'Cause I know you didn't leave that door unlocked." Keith practically growled the words.

"Not a clue." Jason rubbed the back of his neck. "You don't think…?" His uncle hadn't broken in, had he? If he had, why?

"I don't know what to think. It's just odd, that's all." Keith lowered his arms and jerked his head toward the door.

Jason faced Melanie and clasped her hands in his. He ducked his chin and peered into her troubled brown eyes. "Let's put the file away and hit the sack. You have a long day tomorrow in the lab." He and his partner had work to do, and he wanted to save Melanie from more stress.

She nodded her agreement. He released her, and she strode into the kitchen to take care of the paperwork.

Once she exited the living room, he turned to his partner. "Keith?"

"I'll check the back of the house. You get the front. We'll confirm this place is secure before Melanie goes to bed."

Jason made his way through his assigned area. He checked the last window near the couch and found it unlocked. He crouched near the glass opening. A small twig, no more than an inch, lay on the floor next to the wall. His housekeeping skills needed help in many areas, but basic vacuuming wasn't one of them. Where had the errant stick come from? He picked it up and planned to toss it in the garbage when he finished securing the house.

He scanned the room one last time. His gaze landed on the front door. How had the door and the window been left unfastened? He glanced at the tiny piece of wood in his hand and searched his memory. No. He knew he'd secured the perimeter when they'd arrived. And with the declining temps, he hadn't opened a window in weeks.

Then how had his uncle gotten in? And what about the twig?

As his grandmother used to say, something smelled fishy.

NINE

Melanie rubbed her sweaty palms on her jeans. The first time she'd been alone in over a week, and every clang or beep of equipment had her jumping. She had a job to do, and if she didn't calm down, her time in the lab would be useless. She inhaled through her nose and blew out air between her lips. Her heart rate slowed. Time to go to work.

Lab coat on, she hunched over the metal table that held the remains of the woman she'd discovered on her first morning in Valley Springs. She glanced at her clipboard and perused the notes from the exhumation. With all the bones accounted for, she arranged them in the proper location, creating a full skeleton. A young teenage female, to be exact. Melanie stood to an upright position and inspected her handiwork. Rolling her neck from side to side, she worked out the knots in her muscles.

Preferring to proceed in a systematic order, thanks to Professor Gaines, who'd drilled that into her brain, she always worked her way from the top downward, but a hole in the back of the skull had halted her examination before she had gotten started. She patted the tray, searching for her magnifying glass while never taking her eyes off the remains.

Ten times the magnification confirmed her suspicions; the damaged bone told her the end of the teen's story. Cause of death—most likely blunt-force trauma. After scooting a stool beside the table, Melanie sat and continued her analysis of the skeleton, making notes on her document.

Two hours later, she stood and arched her back, stretching the sore muscles. Her spine cracked like the popular rice cereal. She rubbed her neck, working out the stiffness. Her injuries had done a number on her. Maybe she should've stayed home a few days to recover. She sighed. Not an option. This teen's death demanded attention, and the family needed closure.

"Hey, Dr. Hutton, need any help?" Daniel stuck his head in through the doorway.

Melanie jolted and grimaced. She really had to tone down her responses. "Actually, yes. You're what? Six feet tall?"

"About that. Five-eleven to be exact."

"Perfect. Unroll those paper towels, grab the tube and come here." She settled onto her stool and placed her clipboard on the tray. She spun to face him.

He shook his head but proceeded to empty the cardboard tube. "Got it. Now what?"

She motioned him over and kneeled with her back to him. "Hit me over the head with it."

"Say what?"

She peered over her shoulder. The young man's eyebrows rose to his hairline.

"It's an experiment. I have a hunch, and I want to prove it."

"You want me to bonk you over the head with this tube?"

"Exactly."

"I don't understand."

"Our Jane Doe had blunt-force trauma to the head. I'm trying to get an estimate of how tall the killer was."

He looked at her as if she'd lost her mind. And maybe she had, but she had a theory to prove. Or at least, she needed to get enough data to make a preliminary conclusion.

"All right, Doc. Here ya go." Daniel smacked the cardboard to the back of her head, then moved to stand beside her. "Well?"

"Do it again, but raise up on your toes this time."

"All right. If that's what you want."

The tube popped on her head again.

"Did ya get what you needed?"

"Sure did. In my opinion, the person who hit this girl is around six foot one." She held out her hands. "Thanks for the assist."

Daniel helped her to her feet. "I can see working with you will be interesting. Anything else?"

"Nope. That's all. Check back later. I'll have some documents that'll need to be delivered to the sheriff's department." The man had no idea of her interesting quirks. The next few months could be fun. She turned back to the metal table with the bones.

"Will do." A soft click signaled Daniel's departure.

Melanie returned to the remains and rubbed her wrists out of habit. White scars mocked her. Her mind spun to her attacker and Laney's killer. The victim on her table could wait; she wanted answers about Laney's murder. Making her way around the table and trays to the small office within the lab, she grabbed the phone.

A soft metallic rattle came from the main room as if someone had jostled a tray.

Melanie leaned forward and peered out the glass that

attached the two areas. Goose flesh rose on her arms. "Hello? Anyone there?" Silence answered her. "Daniel?" Still nothing.

Her heart rate kicked up a notch. She blew out a long breath. No one had entered the lab; she would've heard them. Her mind had played a trick on her. She shook off the odd sensation and placed a call to the ME.

"Hello?"

"Dr. Vogel? This is Melanie Hutton."

"Dr. Hutton, how can I help you?" His brusque tone made her cringe. She'd have to work on bridging the rift between them if she stayed in Valley Springs. She froze. When had she considered staying? All along, she'd planned to find Allie and go back to the city. Away from the childhood memories and away from the man who'd turned his back on her. But now?

"You still there?"

"Um, yeah, sorry." She'd revisit her new revelation later. "I'm curious if you've finished Laney's autopsy?"

"I have. Not sure why you want a copy, but whatever. Do you want the photos or the report?"

Well, that was a shock. "Both, if you don't mind." She held her breath.

"Emailing it to you as we speak. Anything else?"

"That's all for now. I have pictures I can reference, but I might call later for the actual evidence."

"I'll talk with you then." He hung up.

With a jiggle of the mouse, the computer came to life. She logged on and checked her email. Sure enough, Dr. Vogel had supplied her with the documents she'd requested. Pushing the print option, she rose from the office chair.

The shiver lingering at the base of her spine worked its way up. Someone was in her lab; she felt it in her bones. She retrieved her cell phone from her pocket and pulled up Jason's number. Why had he and Keith decided to leave her alone today? But she'd relied on them too much, and right now, she was being ridiculous. With the lab located next to the sheriff's station and security at every entrance, she was safe. If so, then why did she have a bad feeling?

Ignoring her paranoia, she stuffed the phone in her lab coat and yanked the photos and documents from the printer. She lowered herself into the office chair and studied the markings on Laney's neck, then looked at Dr. Vogel's notes. Laney had lacerations on her head, a blow hard enough to knock her unconscious. But the cause of death—strangulation. Just as Melanie had suspected.

The recent events tumbled through her mind. The fire, Laney's murder and the attempts on her own life. Not until her assailant had vowed to finish what he'd started had she known for sure. But now? Whoever had abducted her was not leaving witnesses alive. Her real-life nightmare was back.

She focused on those days of imprisonment and tried with everything in her to remember, but the truth remained out of reach.

Frustrated at her inability to pull the information from her brain, she rolled back the chair and stood. Striding from the small office space, she returned to the remains. Melanie put aside her own pain. The young girl needed her full attention. She tilted her head and focused on the unknown victim. Hollow orbs in the skull stared back at her. At times during her job, the bones seemed to speak. She threw up a prayer to God for clarity, then returned her attention to the skeleton in front of her.

Tell me your secrets.

Letting her mind wander, she allowed her gaze to

travel up and down the woman's remains. The hair on the back of her neck prickled. Her gaze darted around the room. Had fear gotten the best of her, or was someone in her lab?

She pulled the phone from her pocket. Her fingers trembled as she hit speed dial for Jason's number.

"Hey, Melanie. How's it going?"

Her mouth opened, but her voice failed to work.

"Melanie? Everything okay?" Jason's normal calm had disappeared.

"I'm here," she croaked.

"What's wrong?"

She cleared her throat. "I need you."

"I'm on my way." Jason disconnected. With the sheriff's station next door, he'd arrive at the lab in a matter of minutes.

What had her on edge? Was it the conclusion she'd just come to about Laney or was someone here with her? Her gaze darted around the room. With her back to the connecting office that she'd exited a few minutes ago, Melanie faced the main door. The silver metal table holding the victim's remains sat before her, and the storage room to her right had the extra table pushed up against it. A sink and counter space by the entrance didn't provide a place to hide, and neither did the glass supply cabinets to her left.

She swung her gaze back to the storage room. The table rested crookedly against the wall. Panic clawed up her throat. Her OCD tendencies in the lab had her aligning not only her instruments and tools, but also tables and chairs. She stared at the anomaly. The scene was off. Her gut told her to leave...now. She dashed for the door.

Whack!

White strips of light flashed in her vision. She crumpled to the floor. The last thing that registered in her brain was Jason's panicked voice calling her name from down the hallway.

"Help me, Jason," she mumbled.

Darkness descended, and she fell into an abyss.

"Melanie!" Jason's instincts told him to hurry. He sprinted to her lab, dodging unsuspecting workers as he raced down the corridor.

The lab door banged shut, and a man dressed in black barreled out and crashed through the Exit Only door at the end of the hallway.

Should he follow?

No. Melanie was his top priority. He came to a halt at the entrance of her work area. Pulling his weapon from his holster, he pressed his back against the wall and eased open the door. His Glock at the ready, he peeked inside.

The air whooshed from his lungs. Melanie lay in a heap on the floor.

Rushing in, he slid to his knees beside her. "Mel?" He brushed the hair back from her face and tucked it behind her ear. Blood covered his hand. Staring at the crimson liquid, his world spun. He'd let down his guard because he thought she'd be safe in the secure county lab. He never should have left her unprotected. Jason sucked in a breath to clear his thinking. "Honey? Please, wake up."

He fumbled for his phone and dialed 9-1-1. "I need an ambulance. County lab. Forensics room two." Not caring that Dispatch wanted him to stay on the line, he hung up and called Keith. "Melanie's down. Suspect escaped out the back. Dressed in all black. Approximately six foot, two hundred pounds."

"On it." The line went dead.

Jason had never felt so alone or helpless. He held Melanie in his arms and rocked back and forth. "Come on, sweetheart. Open your eyes." He pulled her in close and cradled her against his chest.

"I can't lose you, too." The realization slammed into him. His heart stopped beating for a moment. "I'm sorry I've been angry for so long. I can't wrap my head around you leaving Allie like that, but I'll learn to deal with it if you'll open those gorgeous brown eyes."

She didn't stir.

He smoothed his hand over her head, exploring the wound.

A knot the size of a walnut and an inch-long gash marked her head. The bleeding hadn't stopped, but it had eased from oozing at an alarming rate.

Boots clomped along the corridor.

Jason drew his gun and pointed it at the entry.

Paramedics Brent and Ethan rounded the corner and came to an abrupt halt.

Ethan raised his hands in surrender. "Whoa, dude. Put that thing away."

After placing his weapon next to his leg, Jason wrapped his arms around his childhood friend.

"Is that Melanie, again?" Brent's shoulders sagged. "That poor lady has really taken it on the chin lately."

"You'll get no argument from me on that one." Jason reluctantly released her into the paramedics' capable hands.

Jason slipped his sidearm back into his holster and paced the small path next to where his friends assessed Melanie. "Is she going to be okay?"

Ethan pulled the stethoscope from his ears and prepped Melanie for transport. "Her vitals are good. Most likely has a concussion. A CT scan will confirm that. She'll have a doozy of a headache and will require a couple of stitches."

"Then why isn't she awake?" Jason squatted beside Brent.

"Dude, she was hit on the head." Brent gave him a *duh* look.

"I know that." Jason ran his hand through his hair. He had to pull it together.

Melanie groaned, and her eyes fluttered open.

"Hey there, Doc. Good to see you again." Ethan smiled at Melanie.

Jason jerked his attention back to her and grabbed her hand. "Mel?"

"Hi." Her whispered response tugged at his heart.

"I hate to interrupt this moment, but we need to get you to the hospital." Brent stood over her and clipped the gurney straps into place.

Melanie closed her eyes and squeezed Jason's hand.

Keith came flying into the room. "How is she?"

Ethan glanced at his partner. "These two are like expectant fathers. Let's get her out of here."

"Brent, stay with her until I get there." Jason watched as the two men raised the gurney and locked it into place.

"Will do. We'll meet you guys at the hospital." Brent jutted his chin toward the door, and he and Ethan hurried out.

Jason stared as his two friends rolled Melanie from the lab. He had to get to the ER. He was not only worried about her condition, but he craved to protect her. *You're a cop, man. Act like one.*

First things first. He spun and met Keith's gaze. "Did you find him?"

"No. No one saw a thing. No strangers prowling about, or men dressed in black."

Jason's breath hitched. "What if this guy is someone we know?"

His partner's head snapped to face him. "Come again?"

"I'm assuming you've been on the same page as me. A stranger among us."

Keith nodded.

"What if it isn't a stranger, but someone from the community? Someone who'd blend in." Jason's stomach turned upside down at the thought. He'd lived with the people of Valley Springs all his life and couldn't fathom any of them being responsible for the attacks and his sister's murder.

"How'd you come up with that?"

"Whoever it is knows this town and the surrounding area well. Think about where this guy buried Laney and where he'd kept Melanie and my sister. Not locations you'd happen upon. Not to mention how he got in here. He has to have connections."

"True." Keith stroked his chin.

"So, who did you see and talk to when you searched for our mystery man?"

Keith narrowed his gaze. "You sure you want to hear this?"

"I'm not sure when you put it that way. But lay it on me." Jason braced himself for his partner's account.

"Sheriff Monroe, Mr. Klein, Sarah from the bakery, Mrs. Horn and your dad."

"My dad? Where was he?" The news twisted his gut like a pretzel.

"Across the street at Lenny's Hardware."

Jason mulled over the information and the five names. Monroe and his dad had both acted strange lately. But so had his uncle Randy. Jason pinched the bridge of his nose. "I don't know what to think. Those are some pretty big accusations. The only thing I am positive of is that Melanie is in the hospital with a gash in her head."

"Don't jump to any conclusions. Let's have solid evidence before we confront anyone."

He nodded. From the names given, he'd do well to remember to have proof before revealing his suspicions. "Speaking of evidence, I want to gather Melanie's current files and documents. Let's take them with us, then lock this place up good and tight."

Keith pulled two sets of nitrile gloves from the box on the counter and tossed him a pair. "Ever get that feeling someone's worried something will trigger Melanie's memory now that she's returned to Valley Springs? Like a smell or voice? You know what I mean?"

"Yup. And the bad part, we have no idea who." Jason snapped on the gloves and exhaled.

He and Keith collected all the papers and photos Melanie had worked on and threw them in a box. Glancing at the skeleton on the table, he withdrew his phone and snapped several pictures for good measure. After a quick scan of the room, he locked the lab door and set the alarm. Anxious to check on her, he hurried to the parking lot.

Keith blocked his path. His partner grabbed the box and tucked the container under his arm. "I'll take the documents to your place. You go on and check on your lady."

"She's not my lady." Not yet, anyway. The more time he spent with her, the more he wanted to take a leap of faith and see if they could get beyond their past.

Keith snorted. "Come on. I'll drop you off at the hospital."

"What about my truck?"

"Dude, it's only a couple blocks away."

"Yeah, right. Kinda forgot about that." Jason rubbed

the back of his neck. His brain had turned to mush. Not a good thing if he intended to be at his best for Melanie.

Keith slapped him on the back. "Let's go, buddy."

Jason hopped into his partner's car and drummed his fingers on the door handle. The image of Melanie bleeding in his arms whirled in his brain. His unfocused mind barely registered the two-minute drive.

"Cooper?" Keith shook his shoulder.

He blinked. "Sorry. Spaced out there for a second."

"I'll say. Go." His partner jutted his chin toward the entrance. "I'll see you at the house. Call me if you need anything."

"Thanks, man." He slid from the seat, closed the car door and tapped the hood.

The ER door whooshed open. Jason stepped inside, tired of stopping at the hospital due to Melanie's injuries. Spotting Dr. Jenson, he jogged to catch up with him. "Doc. Hold up."

Jenson greeted him and shook his hand. "You here for Ms. Hutton again?"

"How is she?" Jason's throat went dry. What if her wounds were worse than Brent and Ethan had thought?

"Other than a mild concussion, three stitches and her previous injuries, she's doing remarkably well."

His lungs deflated. *Thank You, God.* "May I see her?"

"Of course. I left her alone a few minutes ago. She's still a bit woozy, but she's been asking about you."

"Wait. Melanie's by herself? Where's Brent or Ethan?" He stood stock-still, dreading the doctor's answer.

"They had to leave. I told Melanie to rest, and I'd check on her in another twenty to thirty minutes."

Jason's pulse raced. "Where is she?"

"Bay three. Jason, she's okay. The sheriff—"

He pushed past the doctor and sprinted for the small exam room.

What if her attacker had found her? Jason should have stayed by her side. He skidded to a stop outside the curtain as a male voice filtered to his ears. He yanked aside the screen.

"Dennis?" Sheriff Monroe stood next to Melanie's bed. His lack of uniform caught Jason off guard. "What are you doing here?"

The man tucked his phone in his pocket. "Nice to see you, too, Cooper. Dispatch called about the lab break-in. I knew you and Young were busy, so I came to keep an eye on Melanie until you arrived."

Monroe seemed to appear out of nowhere every time she'd gotten hurt. And what about the night of the fire? The man had gasoline on his pants. However, he'd had a plausible explanation.

The implications put Jason on edge. He and Dennis had a friendship that dated back to their preteen years. At times, Monroe's status as his boss gave way to awkward encounters, but overall, they'd maintained an easygoing relationship. He hated the idea of Dennis not being the man he believed him to be.

Setting aside his mistrusting thoughts, he stepped into the room. "How's she doing?"

"Not too bad." The sheriff approached him.

"Has she woken up yet?"

"Yes. I had a quick conversation with her before she fell back asleep."

Jason really should be grateful for his boss to show up and watch out for her. But after toying with the possibility that Melanie's attacker was someone they knew, Jason wouldn't blindly trust, and the sheriff's recent behavior had been suspect. Jason couldn't rule out his boss.

However, since he didn't have anything more than suspicions, no use rocking the boat until he did.

"Thanks for rushing over. I appreciate it. Keith and I surveyed the scene, then locked up the lab."

Dennis squeezed his shoulder. "No problem. Keep me in the loop."

"I will. Looks like she'll be out of commission for a few days—"

"Relax, Cooper. I don't want my newest employee in danger. You and Keith are on protection duty and are authorized to work from home until Melanie can return to the office."

"Thank you, sir."

Monroe grinned at Jason's formal term and patted him on the back. "Any time, my friend." Then he strolled out of the room.

The stress drained from Jason's body. He'd planned to request time off to safeguard Melanie, but Dennis had prevented the need by giving him permission to work from home and assigning him and Keith as her personal bodyguards. One concern taken care of. Now to find out who had tried to kill her.

Whatever disinfectant they used in a hospital needed to change. Each time Jason came, it churned his stomach. The aroma had become an all-too-familiar association with Melanie. Jason scooted the hard plastic chair next to her bed and gripped her hand through the rails. He rested his cheek on the cool metal.

"I'm sorry for letting you down. It won't happen again. I promise." He swallowed past the lump in his throat. He had become attached to the woman he'd vowed to hate. "Come on, Mel. Please, wake up and show me you're okay."

As a big brother, he'd come up short, but he refused

to fail the woman he'd loved as a teen and had turned his back on. Time to face the fact that his heart was fully committed. Someone just needed to tell his brain.

Lord, help me let go of my resentment and be the man she deserves. And help me find her attacker before it's too late.

TEN

The couch cushions enveloped Melanie, and she hadn't moved for the past twelve hours. Jason had tried convincing her that the bedroom would be more comfortable when they'd arrived at his house, but the idea of being alone in a confined space terrified her. At least the living room gave her a sense of security since the guys were never far from sight.

Jason had sat by her side, taking care of her until the doctor had reluctantly signed her release.

Realizing that Jason was just as exhausted as she was, Keith had taken the night shift, insisting Jason get his "beauty rest." She'd have to thank Keith later, but right now, she wanted to strangle him. His attempts to stay quiet had her nerves on edge. Aware of every movement, she'd almost begged him to quit stalking around and make some noise.

The morning sun peeked through the blinds, stirring her from a fitful sleep. Jason's murmured conversation with Keith signaled the changing of the guard. She snuggled farther into the blanket. Her muscles relaxed, and calmness flooded her body. She trusted Keith, but the comfort of daylight and Jason's presence lulled her into a deep slumber...

Hollow eyes stared at her, and a man's rancid breath made her gag. She struggled against the restraints on her wrists. A silver knife blade glinted in the light. The man held the weapon to her throat. She whimpered as the sharp edge dug into her skin. She was going to die.

Her scream pierced the air. She jolted awake and bolted from the sofa.

Feet pounded on the wood floor behind her.

Her breaths came in ragged pants, and she dropped to the floor beside the couch. She scanned the area, searching for something to arm herself.

Jason burst into the room, gun in hand. His gaze landed on her.

She was aware of her surroundings but lacked the ability to focus.

Keith appeared seconds later, his weapon at the ready. "What happened?"

"Unsure." Jason approached her as if soothing a wild animal.

The nightmare lingered, but Jason's voice pulled her to reality. Her teeth chattered, and her body shook.

Jason crouched next to her and scooped her hands into his. "Bad dream?" he whispered.

Unable to put her fears into words, she nodded. His warm touch was a balm to her skittering pulse.

"Go on back to bed, Keith. I've got this." His calloused hand smoothed the sweaty hair from her forehead. "Calm down, honey."

She gasped, powerless to piece together his disjointed words. Struggling to pull in air, she whimpered. "He. Knife." Her thoughts refused to gel. Melanie's hands flew to her throat. No cut. No blood. Her stomach roiled.

"It was only a nightmare. Take a deep breath."

She covered her mouth and swallowed the rising bile.

"How can I help?"

Her gaze landed on his pained emerald-green eyes—she'd never thought she'd be able to look into them again. Blowing out a breath between pursed lips allowed her heart rate to slow.

"It's okay, I've got you." He cupped her cheeks, then pulled her into his chest.

Inhaling his musky cologne, she burrowed into his flannel shirt. Safe and secure in his strong arms. She never wanted to leave.

Minutes later, Jason pulled back and stood. He held out his hands.

She accepted his offer, and he helped her onto the couch. Resting her head on the pillow, she let exhaustion take over. She wouldn't sleep—couldn't sleep—but having Jason close allowed her to relax. She drifted in and out of sleepy consciousness for the rest of the morning.

Since her horrible dream hours ago, Jason had smothered her with concern. Each time she stirred, he hovered. During her early teens, he'd protected her and worried about her. He'd walk her home after dark and tucked her safely inside the house when her parents hadn't cared enough to check on her. She'd believed he'd taken on the role of big brother, but now that she thought about it, maybe it had been more.

"Are you doing okay?" Jason kneeled beside her.

She shifted to face him. "I'd be better if you wouldn't ask every thirty minutes." She smiled, then grimaced. Even smiling hurt.

He tucked a strand of hair behind her ear. "I'm worried about you."

"If it makes you feel any better, I'm worried about me, too." Her reactions and injuries had her jumping at every shadow in the house.

"No. It doesn't." He frowned.

As if her hand had a mind of its own, she reached out and smoothed the crease between his eyebrows. "I'll heal. But I confess, I'd rather not be injured anymore."

He gave her a sad smile and tweaked her nose. "Keith and I promise we'll make every effort to make that a reality."

"Thank you." She shifted to relieve the pressure on her hip. "I'm sick of lying here. Why don't you grab Allison's file, and we can brainstorm? Maybe we can figure out who's attacking me and, at the same time, discover who killed Allie." Time to put an end to this insanity.

After sustaining the hit on the head, her memory, for lack of a better word, fluttered. Images had appeared and vanished so quickly she debated if they were real or her brain had created its own reality. She gritted her teeth. She knew what she had to do. Time to rip off the Band-Aid and face the unpleasant thoughts and feelings, and finally remember details of her abduction and Allison's subsequent disappearance.

"You should rest and not strain yourself. Let Keith and I continue our investigation," he pleaded with her.

"You're not one hundred percent, and you're working—protecting me. Look. I need to remember—*have* to remember—what happened during those two days fifteen years ago. I came back to Valley Springs on a promise to Allie that I'd find her body and put the man responsible behind bars."

Arms crossed over his chest, he sat on his haunches and set his jaw. "You haven't been able to recall anything since you escaped. Why do you think you'll be able to now?"

The jab hurt. The guilt of it all gnawed at her. Had she purposely not remembered to avoid the pain, or had her brain decided to protect her from the trauma? What choice did she have? She had a killer to find. "I have to." She rubbed her temples. "I have focused my whole career and life on this point."

"I understand what you mean by that. I chose to become a detective because of my sister." Jason's tone softened, and he wiped a hand down his face.

"Then let's solve my and Allie's case and put it behind us once and for all." She bit her bottom lip. Would he agree? Or would he push her away? She held out hope he'd find a way to move beyond his assumptions of her role in Allison's death for good.

Jason cupped the sides of her face. "Only if you promise you'll stop if it gets to be too much."

The tenderness in his gaze and in his touch melted her heart. "Deal." The tension in her shoulders eased. She steadied her breathing while Jason disappeared into his office.

His bouncing attitude confused her. The kind, sweet man made her want to weep with hope, but the sour, angry man that occasionally popped out sent her mind reeling.

Jason returned and slid his hand along the back of the sofa, pulling her from her thoughts.

He skirted the couch and placed a thick file on the coffee table. "You saw the documents and pictures earlier. I don't have anything else. Not sure it will do any good, but we can take another look. We do have the information on your recent attacks, so it's worth a shot." He extended his hand and wiggled his fingers.

Accepting the help, she swung her legs over the side of the cushions. The room spun. She bowed her head and begged for the vertigo to stop. The bump on her head had affected her more than she cared to admit. Slowly, she sat upright and released a sigh of relief.

"You look a little green around the edges. Maybe you should listen to the doc and rest."

Jason lowered himself beside her.

"No. I want to get this guy." She didn't care how badly her head hurt, or that her vision wobbled, she refused to lie around and do nothing with a killer on the loose.

Jason continued to study her. His intense gaze seared her skin.

She gathered her courage and cleared her throat. "Come on. Let's do this."

Placing the open file in her lap, he leaned in. "Where do you want to start?"

The same musky cologne he'd worn as a teen teased her nostrils. She'd loved him back then for his kindness and the strong supportive young man he'd been. Now? She once again had fallen for his protective, caring ways. She gently shook her head to dislodge the thought.

"The report. I want to refresh my memory. What there is of it, anyway." The words on the page were hazy, and focusing was impossible, thanks to her concussion. "Could you read it to me? My brain doesn't want to co-operate."

He took the paper from her and read the report written by the detective assigned to the case.

A recall of the basic details wasn't the problem. The problem was that the police only had fundamental facts, nothing beyond Melanie's own recollection. They did, however, have the location of her captivity and the evidence recovered from the scene. The place she had no desire to return to. The place that haunted her dreams. A small, damp cabin in a sea of thick trees. No one around to hear her screams.

"Remember anything?" He didn't rush her, just sat patiently, and waited.

Tears welled. "Nothing more than what's in the report." And a sense of evil that surrounded the events.

Removing the file from her lap, he shuffled the contents. "Ready to look at the pictures?"

Sure, why not. This had been her idea, after all. "Hand them over."

Jason deposited the stack into her hands. He rubbed her upper back between her shoulder blades. "Take your time."

She sucked in a ragged breath and looked down. Her battered face stared back at her. She feathered her fingers over the image. The split lip. The swollen eye. The black-and-blue marks from her cheekbone to her jawline. "He did a number on me, didn't he?"

"Yes, he did." Jason grasped her hand and squeezed.

If she accepted his comfort, she'd never finish the task. She pulled away and flipped to the next photo.

The dingy cabin sat before her. The memories sat below the surface. Her stomach roiled. If she could reach through the fog, grasp hold and pull them out, they might discover the missing pieces to the puzzle.

"You said that Allison told you to go get help if you ever got free." The sharp edge of his voice had her recoiling.

She nodded. That conversation was the only clear recall of the events her brain had.

"Your wrists were tied together, right?"

"Yes." She'd never allowed herself to mentally go back to that horrible place. Her therapist had told her that she needed to heal first, but how could she if her mind mimicked Swiss cheese? She had to relive the memories if she ever wanted to move on. She rubbed the invisible sores on her wrists.

Jason clasped her forearms. "It's okay, Mel. You're safe."

She peered at him and gave a forced smile. "I know."

"Has your therapist ever tried hypnotherapy?"

"No. We tried EMDR—eye movement desensitization and reprocessing. And it helped with my PTSD symptoms, but it never brought back my memories. I refused hypnosis. As much as I wanted to remember, I couldn't force myself to go back there at the time. Now?" She'd committed to finding Allie's body and that meant discovering the identity of their abductor. What choice did she have? "I guess it's time to face my fears." She'd call her therapist and set up an appointment.

Jason dipped his head and peered into her eyes. "Do you trust me?"

She furrowed her brow. "Of course."

"I may not be a psychologist, but I have training on how to help witnesses remember. Sometimes when they're overwhelmed, I have to walk them through it. Now that you're older, and it isn't so fresh, will you let me try?"

All she could do was nod. This is why she'd come home, to put it all behind her.

"Okay, here we go." His Adam's apple bobbed. "Close your eyes."

Her heart pounded. "I—I can't." Seeing it with her eyes open was one thing, but to have it visit her dream…

"Yes, you can," he demanded, then softened his voice. "Please, try."

Lowering her eyelids, she swallowed past the lump in her throat. She could do this—had to do this. For herself, for Allison, for Jason.

"Picture yourself in the cabin." He paused and ran his thumb over the white scars from the bindings that had marred her wrists. "Where were you?"

The musty room closed in on her. She slid her hand into Jason's and clamped down. His support gave her the strength to go on. She mentally returned to the cabin that had changed her life forever. The summer humidity made it hard to breathe. Her muscles ached, and her battered body throbbed. The grime on the floor and stench in the air churned her stomach. "On the floor. My wrists were tied together with zip ties."

"Could you get away?" Jason's words echoed through a long tunnel.

The cabin walls appeared before her. She sat on hard wood and tugged on the restraints. "No. There was a rope attached to the ties that anchored me to the wall."

"Where was Allie?"

"I don't want to look." Terrified of what she'd find, Melanie dipped her chin. She didn't want to look around the room. Didn't want to see the horrors around her.

"Allie needs you, Mel. Where is she?"

Caught between the present and the past, Melanie sucked in a harsh breath. "Next to me."

"Can you reach her?"

"No. Allie's on the other side of the fireplace," she squeaked. Her mind refused to release the details, but the feeling of something terribly wrong twisted her gut. Desperation to help Allie swamped her.

"Shh. It's okay. Now, tell me about when Allison told you to escape."

She gripped his hand hard enough to break his fingers. Tears trickled down her cheeks. "She told me if I could, to run—to go get help."

"How did you get free from your restraints?"

A whimper spilled from her lips. "Someone helped me."

"Allie?"

Melanie whipped her head from side to side. Her eyes popped open. She jerked away her hands. "I'm sorry, Jason. I'm so sorry." Memories flooded her brain. Identities and specifics continued to elude her, but of one thing, she was certain.

"Honey, who helped you?" He smoothed a hand over her hair.

"I don't know. But—" Melanie's cries filled the air. "Allie was already dead."

Tears pooled on his lashes. He wrapped Melanie in his arms, pulled her into his chest and let her cry.

Her guilt from leaving her friend behind had been for nothing. Any lingering sliver of hope that Allison had survived had vanished.

No more doubts—Allie was dead.

All these years, Jason thought Melanie had left Allison in the hands of a killer. Now he knew differently. Melanie had been with his sister when she died. Probably watched as Allie took her last breath.

"I'm sorry you had to go through that." Maybe he shouldn't have pushed, but she'd remembered more than the report had said. Another person out there had information. Finding an unknown witness presented a new challenge.

She slapped at the tears. "I hate that I can't remember everything. If I could, the man responsible would be rotting in jail."

He cupped her cheek, and she leaned into his touch. "We'll figure it out—together."

"I like the sound of that." She exhaled and winced.

"Need your pain meds?" He shifted and grabbed the pill bottle from the side table.

"Might be a good idea." She accepted the container and took the medication. Resting back against the couch, she closed her eyes. "Did I see that you brought my files from the lab?"

"Sure did. Keith and I wanted them somewhere safe, so we brought the documents here."

"You didn't grab the photos from the desk, did you?" She raised an eyebrow and peeked at him through tiny slits.

"Of course." He grinned. Even battered and in pain, Melanie had a mischievousness that he adored.

Her shoulders relaxed. "Good. Now that we know my attacks, the kidnapping and Laney's murder are tied together, I want to take a closer look at the ME's report." Creases formed on her forehead.

Her furrowed brow worried him. He wanted her to remember not just for his sake, but for hers, too. How awful it must be to lose two significant days of your life. He sat in silence, allowing her time to process the new memories. And his brain craved a moment to wrestle with the timing of Allison's death.

A few minutes later, he brushed the back of his hand over Melanie's cheek. "Feel like sitting at the table? Or do you want to rest?"

"I need to get up. My head is demanding I take it easy, but the rest of me is screaming to move. I feel like I'm a hundred years old."

"That stiff, huh?"

She nodded with caution.

"Then let's get you walking around a bit." He wiggled his fingers. He shouldn't push, but keeping her busy seemed like a prudent move. He'd keep a watchful eye on her, and at the first sign of overdoing it, he'd stop the investigation and insist she take a nap.

She accepted his invitation and rose to her feet with a groan. "This is ridiculous."

He chuckled at her scowl. "Come on, we'll take it slow."

"*Slow* is not in my vocabulary," she grumbled.

"Well, it is now." He pinched his lips together to keep from laughing. Same old Melanie, always going Mach 1 in everything she did.

"You're enjoying this, aren't you?" She focused her attention on the walk around the room.

Jason wondered if her question had a double meaning. His anger had propelled a desire to never speak to Melanie again, but his heart had betrayed him. In no way did he relish her struggle with injuries. In fact, he'd take on her pain if he could. Now that he knew the order of events, shame for accusing Melanie had blanketed him like a storm cloud.

Should he say something or let her comment go? He'd take it like the jest she'd offered.

"Never." He waggled his eyebrows.

"You never could lie." She shifted and stared at him. "Jason. I knew you were hurting. And it hurt to think you blamed me, but I never held it against you. I blamed myself for surviving, and then when I couldn't remember..." Tears glimmered in her eyes.

"Oh, Mel. The amnesia isn't your fault. Maybe I had thought you were holding out on me, but not anymore." He stopped her and tucked a flyaway hair behind her ear. "I think it's time we give ourselves a little grace." He knew she'd never fully forgive him for being such a jerk when she needed him the most, but he could offer the proverbial olive branch and recapture their friendship.

"That sounds lovely." Melanie took a deep breath and let it out slowly. "Show me the files, and let's get to work."

Jason led her into the kitchen and pulled out a chair. "Hold on." He hurried to the living room and grabbed a pillow. "Here. No reason for you to sit on a wooden seat."

She lowered herself on the cushioned chair and smiled up at him. "Thanks."

His gaze landed on the open blinds. He'd closed the blinds in the main room to obscure the view, but not in the kitchen. No need to invite Melanie's attacker to take a shot at her through the glass. He strode to the windows and twisted the rod, closing the slats.

"Please leave them open. It feels like a cave in here."

"Sorry, but I'm not taking any chances with you. This guy's getting bolder, and I refuse to give him another opportunity."

She sighed. "I can't live like this. Something has to give."

He drew a chair close to her and sat down. "Focus on what we can do. The rest will work itself out." He handed her the file. "Why don't we put aside the kidnapping for a bit. Give yourself a little distance from that piece. It might give you a new perspective."

Melanie rubbed her forehead. "You might be right." Without another word, she opened the file and spread the contents in front of her. He sensed her frustration at being closed in, but chose to ignore it. Her safety was the only thing that mattered.

"What are we looking for?" He picked up a photo and examined it.

"Clues."

"Well, duh. I meant what kind."

She glanced at him. Redness rimmed her eyes. "I

know Laney's cause of death, but I want to take a closer look at the other traumas to the body, along with anything else that I might have missed."

"Works for me."

Melanie remained quiet—too quiet—as she stared at the papers.

He clutched her hand. "I'll take notes, and you do what you do best."

She snorted. "I sift through dirt and examine bones."

"You take puzzle pieces and make sense out of them. It's no different than finding missing bones and creating a full skeleton to discover how someone died." He released her and pointed to the stack.

She nodded and lifted the pictures. Her eyebrows pinched together. "These are of each stage of the exhumation." She continued a slow flip through the photos and paused on the fourth one. "Check out the lacerations on her cranium."

He squinted and focused on the marks. "Okay." He knew she was getting at something, so he waited for her to continue.

"I noticed this before. I'm thinking the tire iron. If not that, then something similar."

Jason touched his head and grinned. "Yeah, I'm familiar with it."

Melanie rolled her eyes and flipped to a new image. "See the bruising on Laney's neck?"

"Yup."

"I agree with Dr. Vogel. The cause of death was strangulation. This was personal." Melanie bit her lip. Her unseeing gaze troubled him.

"Mel, what's wrong?"

"I don't know, but something triggered the spark of memory."

"What was it?"

"That's just it—I'm not sure."

He rubbed the back of his neck. Melanie's instincts had served her well…so far. "There must be something to it. Talk it out."

A frown marked her face. "I can't get the glimpses of Allison out of my mind, and I can't get the full memory to return. It's like my brain is torturing me. There's a clue in Laney's death, I can feel it. I just can't figure out what it is."

"A sound, a smell, a person?"

Tipping her head back, she gazed at the ceiling. Her eyes darted back and forth as if searching for the answer.

She jolted upright. "Sickening sweet."

"What?"

"A sweet smell."

"As in candy?"

"No. More of an odor."

"Where did you notice it?"

Her shoulders slumped. "On Laney's clothes, I think. Maybe the hospital, too? Or the station? I have no idea."

Any place Melanie had visited had become a possibility.

How was he supposed to find the guy and put an end to all this?

Melanie dropped her head into her hands. If she could only latch on to where. "What am I going to do? If I don't figure this out, he's not going to stop hunting me."

"I don't know, honey. I'm worried. But Keith and I will do everything in our power to protect you." He placed his finger under her chin and lifted. "I've spent so much time letting my anger control my thinking, but I can't deny I care about you…a lot. I refuse to let anything happen to you." He tugged her into his arms.

She nestled into his embrace. Ever since she turned fourteen, she'd waited for him to admit he liked her for more than a little sister. Even though he hadn't declared his love, the fact he cared *a lot* warmed her heart. *I fell for you a long time ago, Jason. It might have been a teenage crush, but it was real to me.* Her muscles ached, and her head throbbed, but she had no intention of moving from his hold.

"Well, well, well. It's about time." Keith, with sleep-mussed hair, padded into the kitchen in his stocking feet .

"Stuff it, partner." Jason released her and glared at Keith.

"Just calling it like I see it." Keith poured himself a cup of coffee. Leaning his hip against the counter, he took a sip and grinned over the rim.

"Come over here and be useful," Jason grumbled.

Melanie bit her lip to hide her smile. Jason and Keith had a great friendship beyond work. Their banter reminded her of two playful bear cubs.

Unwilling to fuel Keith's assumption, Melanie motioned to the chair next to her. "We think we've made a connection."

"I can see that." Keith sat and sipped his drink.

"Knock it off, dude." Jason huffed.

"Show me what you've got."

She related their findings, including the memory of the sweet scent, while Jason jumped in, adding details when necessary. The tag-team description, a smooth presentation. They really did work well together.

Keith rubbed his stubbled jaw. "You have my attention. Can you physically tie Laney, Melanie's attacker and Allison together?"

"No." Jason spoke on top of Melanie's "Maybe."

Keith arched an eyebrow, and the corner of his mouth lifted. "You two want to compare notes on that and try again?"

Melanie took charge. "We can't locate Allison's remains without discovering who abducted us, and until my memory returns in full, we are no closer to that answer. As for Laney... I truly believe she unknowingly stumbled onto the person who set my apartment on fire. She probably never put the two events together, but the killer got nervous and couldn't take that chance. If we delve deeper into her murder, instead of looking into the past, we might find who we're looking for." She shrugged.

Jason considered her for a moment. "Still a lot of unanswered questions, but I like the theory. Let me grab my laptop so I can log in and look at the fire report. Keith, why don't you check in with Kyle?" He pushed from the table at the same time his phone rang. He held up a finger. "Hello?" His brow furrowed. "No, I haven't talked with Dad."

What happened now? She gave him a questioning look.

He pointed to the phone and mouthed *Uncle Randy*.

Melanie's heart sank. If Randy couldn't locate Ben, then Jason's dad was drinking again.

"Look, Uncle Randy, I'm in the middle of something and can't leave right now." Jason stepped outside on the back porch. His voice trailed off, and the door clicked shut behind him.

"That doesn't sound good." Keith's gaze stayed on the closed door.

"How bad has it been?" She hadn't realized how serious the situation had gotten since Allison's disappearance. When she left Valley Springs, she focused on the aftereffects of her abduction that pertained to her, and had never considered what Jason had experienced beyond losing his sister. He'd turned his back on her, and she hadn't had the mental capacity to do anything except survive.

"Bad enough that Jason's had to leave work several times a week to pick his dad up from the bar during the day."

"I had no idea," she whispered. Granted, her own life had taken a nosedive, but the fact she hadn't checked on Jason? Her selfishness stung. "I should have been a better friend."

Her aching muscles required a change of positions. She stood and stretched, wincing at the movement. Unable to help herself, she ambled to the window. With two fingers, she lifted a slat in the blinds and peered out at Jason.

He ran a hand through his hair as he paced the length of the porch. Head down and shoulders slumped, he portrayed a picture of dejection. The man had the burdens of the world pressing down on him.

"You shouldn't be standing there," Keith warned.

She glanced at Keith. "I know, but I haven't seen the light of day since I got here." She returned her focus to the man who had captured her heart. "Plus, I'm worried about him."

Jason hung up and stared off into the backyard. He jerked his gaze toward her. "Get down!" He jumped in front of the window.

A shot blasted in the air.

Melanie cried out. Dropping to the ground, she covered her head with her arms as glass rained down.

Keith sprinted to the door, flung it open and crawled outside.

Melanie raised to her hands and knees. Crystal-like

pieces tumbled from her hair and back. On shaky legs, she hunched over. Glass crunched under her feet as she made her way to the door and peeked around the edge.

Keith grabbed Jason by the back of the shirt and dragged him toward the door.

The blood trail that smeared across the wooden surface claimed her ability to think.

"Move!"

She scrambled out of Keith's path and stared at the man bleeding in front of her.

Keith pulled Jason inside. "Close the door."

Her trembling limbs struggled to obey. She slammed the door shut and hurried to Jason's side.

"Hang in there, partner." Phone to his ear, Keith notified the station. "Annie, I need backup at Jason's house." He slid his duty weapon from the holster and hurried from the room.

Melanie bent and kissed Jason's temple. "Please be okay."

His eyes flitted open. He clutched his upper arm and groaned.

The blood oozing between his fingers stole her breath. Jason had taken a bullet because of her stupid need to look outside. "I'm so sorry." When would this insanity stop? Heart in her throat, Melanie caressed his cheek. "Try to relax."

Jason shook his head. "Help me up." With her assistance, he struggled to sit up and scooted to the kitchen cabinet. Leaning back, he drew in a long breath.

"Jason, please don't move anymore." She smoothed his hair from his forehead. He'd looked after her, now she planned to take care of him.

Pulling in a cleansing breath, she focused on the problem at hand. She had to stop the bleeding. Melanie hunched over the counter and grabbed a towel. She lowered herself beside Jason and pressed the cloth against his wound.

He sucked in a ragged breath and took over holding the fabric.

Out of breath, Keith slipped into the kitchen and holstered his Glock. He crouched next to Jason. "Whoever it was is gone. Want to tell me what happened?"

She covered Jason's hand and answered Keith's question. "Someone tried to shoot me, and Jason jumped in the way."

Keith's gaze darted between them.

Jason shrugged and winced. "It seemed like the thing to do."

Tears threatened to fall. If she hadn't stepped to the window… "It was stupid of me. I'm responsible for you getting hurt."

He waved his hand, dismissing her thought. "Let's not play the blame game. We've done that for far too long."

How could she not take responsibility for his injury? The man's resentment hadn't kept him from sacrificing himself for her. But then again, hadn't they moved past the old feelings of bitterness?

Keith's phone buzzed. "Looks like the cavalry has arrived." He pointed his gaze at Jason. "Ambulance?"

"Nope."

"Stay put." He answered the call and tromped to the front door.

Melanie's attention turned to Jason. His clenched teeth and creased brow spoke of the pain he had to be experiencing.

She lifted the towel. "Looks like it ripped a groove in your skin. You need stitches."

Without lifting his head from the cabinet door, Jason rolled his head from side to side and met her gaze.

"Not going. I'm not leaving you. First-aid kit is under the sink. Wash it out and butterfly it shut."

"Jason. You need to go to the hospital." Melanie entwined her fingers with his blood-covered ones, the sticky substance a reminder of his heroic actions and her stupidity.

"No. I need to keep you safe." His determined gaze bored into her.

For all the times he'd stood up for her, he deserved her support. Helpless to do much else, she'd stand beside him. She rummaged in the cabinet and found the kit. After filling a bowl of water and grabbing extra towels, she cleaned his wound and used the emergency laceration closures from the bag to seal the gash.

She wetted a couple of towels and helped him wipe his hands clean. "I'd advise taking something for the pain. Once the shock wears off, you're gonna hurt."

"Too late." Jason forced a smile and grimaced.

She brushed her hand along his jaw. "I am so sorry."

He leaned into her touch. "Please don't apologize."

Keith stomped into the room and jammed his fists on his hips. "My partner got shot, and Melanie has more injuries than I can count. This has to stop."

Someone was targeting her, and the attacks were centered on her and Allie's abduction. The answers to Allison's death were locked in her brain. Deep down, she knew what she had to do.

Sweat beaded on her forehead. She swallowed hard. "Take me to the cabin."

"No. I won't put you out in the open for this guy to kill you." Jason clasped her arm. "Not to mention the trauma of visiting where he held you captive."

It hadn't escaped her that she'd be in the killer's cross-hairs, but it didn't matter anymore. She refused to have Jason's death on her conscience. "One way or the other, I have to force myself to remember every painful detail."

"And if he kills you?" Horror laced Jason's expression.

"Then you'll arrest him and make him pay." Her statement held more confidence than she possessed, but as Keith said, it had to stop.

ELEVEN

Melanie opened the passenger door of Jason's truck but didn't move. Her nerve endings sparked. For the first time since she'd announced her plans, doubt crept in.

A hint of snow infused the air, and dried leaves rustled on the ground. Melanie sat and stared at the tiny, abandoned hunting cabin that haunted her dreams. After she'd escaped, and the police had investigated, she discovered that the structure was on county property. Hunters stumbled upon it from time to time, but there was no owner to tie it to.

She willed herself to continue, but her legs had turned to liquid, and her hands trembled. She struggled to rein in her racing pulse. Her instincts screamed at her to run away. How would she walk into that place?

Jason appeared in front of her. He hugged his injured left arm against his midsection. "Don't get out. Keith is clearing the area."

She nodded. Not a problem; she had no desire to leave his vehicle. Her heart thumped like a bass drum. She wiped her sweaty palms on her jeans.

"Hey, it's okay. I won't leave your side." He placed his hand on her knee.

The connection with him grounded her. She'd dealt

with the trauma years ago, but without a full memory, there were events she hadn't come to terms with. Happenings, she feared, that waited to drag her under emotionally and never release her.

Keith rounded the small structure and strode toward them. His gaze darted along the perimeter of the tree line. "All clear. I'll stand guard while you two do your thing."

Jason extended his right hand.

She sucked in a ragged breath, accepted his help and slid from the truck. Her knees buckled. Jason gripped her tight, steadying her. Melanie's body refused to move. The desire to hop back into the vehicle and drive away overwhelmed her. She hadn't returned to Valley Springs, let alone this building, in fifteen years. Her only memories of the cabin held confusion and terror. The location, Allie telling her to go for help if she got free and recently her best friend's lifeless eyes boring into her. A sight she longed to forget.

Jason's hands rested on her waist. He dipped his chin and peered at her. "What can I do to help?"

Take me far away from here. A tear trailed down her cheek, and she swiped it away. She had no choice. She owed it to Allie to expose her killer. Owed it to Jason and herself. They both needed closure.

Shoulders back, she inhaled. "Stay with me."

"I'll be right by your side the whole time." He kissed her cheek. "Okay?"

She bit her lower lip and nodded.

Keith stood like a sentinel, weapon in hand. The man's gaze swept back and forth, ready for an attack.

The wind had kicked up, and leaves swirled in the air. Locks of Melanie's hair whipped across her face. She hooked them with her pinkie, scooped them from her mouth, then tucked the stray hairs behind her ear. The two-room cabin sitting in the middle of a small clearing surrounded by woods had her imagination working overtime. Was someone out there watching, waiting? She scanned the area and tried to rub the chill from her arms. Exhaling, she returned her focus to the small building. The left side of the front porch had caved in. She slogged toward the structure and up to the steps. One of the three had rotted, leaving a gaping hole.

A shiver snaked up her spine. Her head spun. She stumbled.

Jason wrapped his good arm around her waist. "I've got you."

Melanie rested her cheek on his chest. The man had been her rock since he'd discovered she hadn't left Allie to die. She prayed that when—if—she remembered everything, she'd still have a chance with him. She wanted to chuckle. How could she think about a future with Jason at a time like this? Catching Allie's killer and staying alive had to stay at the forefront of her mind.

The injuries she'd sustained since her return to Valley Springs chose that moment to flare in intensity. Her head and ankle throbbed, not to mention the pain from all the bumps and bruises scattered over her body. She swallowed the bile rising in her throat.

Lord, help me. I can't do this without You.

The verse her aunt whispered to her every time Melanie had a panic attack swirled in her mind. *I can do all things through Christ which strengthen me.* Her aunt had passed away five years ago. The only person in her life who'd given her unconditional love had been there one minute and gone the next. Oh, how she wanted her aunt with her right now.

She'd lost so much over the years. Her parents had never cared, not really. Their careers and reputation had meant more to them than their own child. Then she'd lost her best friend and the man beside her all in one swoop. Aunt Heather had taken her in and shown her God's love. When her aunt's heart attack at the age of fifty-two had taken Melanie by surprise, she had God to lean on. And had every day since.

Fingers entwined with Jason's, Melanie climbed the steps and placed her hand on the doorknob. She pushed open the door. A musty odor tickled her nose. She cleared her throat and continued her trek into the cabin. Dust danced in the beams of light, shining through the grimy windows. The remnants of a tattered old brown couch rested in the middle of the room. A small kitchen table set at an odd angle, one of the legs broken. Her gaze darted to the two closed doors. Her memory clicked. A bathroom and a bedroom.

The door clunked, closing behind her.

She jumped.

"Sorry." Jason's voice echoed in the old cabin.

Wrapping her arms around her waist, she absorbed the evil that filled the room. Evil she'd lived. She staggered to the rock fireplace and kneeled next to a steel loop. She slid her fingers over the metal. An image of a man standing above her flashed through her mind. She gasped and jerked from the cold silver as if it had burned her.

"Mel?" Jason's concern tugged at her heart.

"I— He—" She stood and stared. Nausea stirred in her belly.

Jason moved to her side and ran a hand down her arm.

She pulled away. "Please don't." Her skin buzzed with electricity. A simple touch seared her nerves.

Jason dropped his hand to his side.

If only she could accept the contact, but she was holding on by a thread. She moved to the other steel loop.

Dark burgundy splatter, obscured by dust, coated the floor and the wall. Tears stung her eyes. She lowered herself to the floor and covered her face; sobs racked her body. The man in her nightmares had killed her best friend in this spot, and she had witnessed the cruelty.

Every scream, every maniacal laugh, tortured her soul. Allie, only five feet away, and Melanie couldn't do a single thing to save her friend. Her heart shattered. She fell into Jason's arms, and he enfolded her in his embrace. Burying her face in his chest, she cried out her pain.

Memories flooded back. Excruciatingly vivid details slammed into her, stealing her breath. Except for the identity of the man who'd held her captive. *Why can't I remember who it was, God?*

An image of a face flashed like lightning. Melanie gasped. "Ben?" No. Not possible.

"What did you say?" Jason eased her back. His eyes had turned dark and suspicious as he looked at her.

Melanie's stomach threatened to empty at the realization that it had been Jason's father that she'd remembered. The image of him hovering over her grew clearer, sharper. He had been there!

"Nothing." She pulled from Jason's embrace and turned away from him, regretting that the name had slipped from her lips. Fifteen years ago, Jason had ripped out her heart when he'd accused her of abandoning Allie. He'd never believe her and accept the truth about his father.

Tears came fast and hard. Not only for the pain of remembering, but also the knowledge she couldn't endure Jason's lack of trust again, or the accusations that were sure to come. The chance of having a future with him had disintegrated in that single memory.

"Why did you say my dad's name?" His voice held a dangerous edge.

The weight of her crushed dreams dropped her heart to the floor.

Why, Ben? Why?

Confusion and rage warred in Jason's mind. When Melanie had spoken his dad's name, his heart shattered, and all that old anger and bitterness toward her came rushing back like a tidal wave threatening his equilibrium. She had to be remembering incorrectly. Or, worse yet…covering up her own guilt at leaving Allie by blaming his father. He had only her word that his sister had been dead when she'd left her. He'd already lost Allie. He wouldn't—he couldn't—allow her to take the only family he had left.

"My dad would never hurt Allison."

"He was there, Jason. I remember seeing him."

She reached for his arm, but he pulled it away, the truth finally dawning on him. She hadn't returned to town to find Allie's killer. She'd come to appease her own guilt at leaving his sister behind no matter who she had to implicate. "You're lying."

"I've never lied to you. I've done nothing but try to be your friend. Aside from Allie, you were always my best friend, Jason."

"Some friend. First, you leave Allison behind, and now you try to implicate my father?"

The color drained from her face. "You're doing it again! Not asking, not listening!" When he didn't budge, fire lit behind her eyes. "Fine. Have it your way. You wanted me to remember. That's why you brought me here, but I should have known you couldn't handle the truth. You aren't the man I thought you were." She stomped out the door and down the steps.

He slapped the wall. The skin on his arm pulled his wound, causing strobe lights to flash behind his eyelids. He blew out a breath between pursed lips. He plodded to the door, then kicked it open. The wood smashed against the exterior, splintering on contact.

His gaze traveled to the passenger seat of his truck. The woman who'd destroyed his trust in her sat with her head back and eyes closed. *Good.* He had no desire to speak with her.

Keith stood at the passenger's side of his car, a stunned expression on his face. "Everything okay?"

"Peachy." He held his left arm cradled against his middle.

Keith jutted his chin at Jason's injury. "Your arm?"

"I'll live."

"Any progress with her memory?" Keith stood, feet apart, and crossed his arms.

Jason gritted his teeth. "I'd say."

"Is it someone we suspected?"

Keith's question startled him, reminding him about his father's presence close by the lab when Melanie had been attacked. And his behavior had been odd lately. Jason opened his mouth but couldn't speak his father's name out loud. That would make this all too real.

The experience had caught up with him. He rested his hip on the car door and ran his hand over his face, thankful his partner didn't push for details.

"Now what?" Keith's words were so quiet, Jason almost didn't hear him.

"I'll take her to the station and get her statement." He wouldn't like it, and he wasn't even certain he would believe it, but it was procedure, and it needed to be done.

"The station? You think she's up for that?"

"She has to be. We have a killer to catch," Jason growled. He rubbed his forehead and prayed Melanie's revelation didn't send his world tumbling down a mountain.

"You head out. I'll follow and meet you in town." Keith straightened and dropped into the driver's seat of his department-issued car.

Jason pushed off the vehicle and trudged to his truck. "See ya there." He slid onto the seat and started the engine. He massaged the muscle under his wound. More ibuprofen was a serious necessity.

Inhaling, he pulled onto the dirt road. For two miles, the truck bumped along, hitting potholes and ruts on the narrow path. He glanced at Melanie, who sat staring out the passenger window. The fading sun shone through the windshield, highlighting the purple bruises that marred her face.

Silence filled the truck cab, neither of them making an effort to thaw the frozen invisible wall between them. He mulled over what she meant when she said his dad's name. He'd never confessed to anyone that he'd questioned his father's role in Allison's disappearance. Shame had consumed him for entertaining the idea that his father could have hurt Allie. With Melanie's whispered declaration of his father's name, he'd lost it. His own guilt had pushed him to blame her once again.

Ben Cooper had become a drunk over the years, requiring more and more of Jason's time and effort. He'd become his father's caretaker. His uncle Randy had helped, but the responsibility had landed on him. His dad never would've hurt Allie. The man loved his daughter—of that, Jason was sure. But doubt lingered.

He refused to accuse his dad of any wrongdoing without evidence. But after witnessing Melanie's reaction, he shouldn't have yelled at her. He should have listened before passing judgment. She was right to call him on that. He'd reacted, allowing his emotions to get the better of him instead of listening to what she had to say. He'd done that once before, and it had been a big mistake, had left him brewing with anger and bitterness for far too long. When they arrived in town, he'd apologize for jumping to conclusions. Assuming she was willing to listen.

His gaze traveled to the beautiful brunette fuming next to him. All these years, he'd imagined her living a wonderful life filled with family and friends, while he'd lost his. His dad to alcohol and his sister to a madman. He had never been so wrong. The woman had survived, thanks only to her aunt's love and influence of faith. And he'd hated her for something she hadn't done. Now she was trying to tell him what had happened, and he had refused to listen. He was such an idiot. He had to make it right before she pushed him away forever.

Attention back on the business of driving, he slowed to a stop at the intersection of the highway. A large snowflake splatted on his windshield. Then another and another in quick succession. It looked like winter had finally arrived.

The intensity of the snowfall increased as he turned and drove south on the county highway. The wipers on his truck worked hard to keep up with the sudden dump of white stuff. His gaze darted in a constant scan of his surroundings. The hairs on the back of his neck prickled. He squinted at his rearview mirror, searching for anything amiss. As if he could see through the nearly blinding snow. The next ten miles—the perfect place to stage an ambush on a clear day—loomed ahead. He sat up straight and gripped the steering wheel, ignoring the discomfort in his arm. His and Melanie's lives depended on his ability to spot danger. His gaze darted to the rear-view mirror. The blanket of white made it impossible to see Keith behind them.

Jason shrugged off the uneasiness and continued his trek.

Ten minutes and he'd have Melanie safely tucked away at the station. He focused on his goal but stayed aware and ready for trouble. He breathed a sigh of relief when he hit the five-mile mark.

The rev of an engine had him searching for the location of the sound. A black truck appeared to his left, crashing into his door. Metal crunched and popped, echoing through the cab of the truck. His head slammed against the driver's-side window. Glass exploded around him.

Sharp edges of the shattered glass cut into his face and slashed into his sleeves. The world turned gray. He pivoted his head and caught a glimpse of Melanie's brown hair tumbling across her face. The truck came to a halt. A dark figure grabbed Melanie. "Mel?" he croaked. He clawed his way through the fog, but darkness descended.

Please keep Melanie safe.

He fell into the abyss of nothingness.

TWELVE

Hands yanked Melanie from her seat. She frantically grappled for anything to stop her fall, but hit the ground with a thud. Sharp rocks pierced her palms and added to the scrapes on her knees. Her head throbbed as if seconds away from exploding. She struggled to open her eyes, but they refused to cooperate.

Fingers to her temples, she whispered, "What happened?"

"You came back. That's what happened. If you'd have stayed away, you'd have lived." The deep baritone voice had a familiarity about it. Her mind reached for clarity but failed.

White dots swirled behind her eyelids. "Where's Jason?" Something had to have happened to him. He'd hurt her by accusing her of lying, but he wouldn't abandon her, would he? No, Jason wouldn't let that stop him. Protectiveness was too ingrained in him.

"That boy couldn't leave well enough alone," the voice growled.

"Please tell me you didn't hurt him." If her eyes would only open and the world would stop spinning.

"He'll survive."

The memory of the crash came roaring back. Melanie

had turned in time to see the blur of a black truck slam into Jason's door. Her stomach churned. Lifting to her hands and knees, she retched. She wiped her mouth and staggered to her feet only to collapse. Pain shot through her hip and shoulder. She whimpered and rolled into a ball. A dark curtain closed over her, and her surroundings disappeared.

Melanie's brain clicked on. A seat belt was fastened across her chest and waist, and the steady hum of a car engine met her ears. She forced her eyes open, but found herself blindfolded. Lifting her hand to tug the cloth away from her face, she realized her wrists were zip-tied in front of her. Her pulse thumped beneath her skin. Images of her and Allie swirled in her mind. Melanie's hands—tied just like they had been fifteen years ago. The link to the past terrified her.

The lump in her throat grew.

"Leave the blindfold. Unless you want me to kill you now," the man snarled.

The choice to either be killed here and now, or held captive and tortured, weighed in her mind. After what she'd endured as a teen, a quick death sounded better. But what if Jason found her in time? Assuming he was alive. No, she'd take her chances and hold out hope for him to come to her rescue. She lowered her trembling hands.

A sharp turn slammed her elbow into the door, sending pain shooting up her arm. Tires crunched on gravel, and the vehicle bounced over grooves in the road. The unrelenting movements jarred her already injured body. She gritted her teeth. At the mercy of the man driving, she focused on his voice. Her brain strained to identify the stranger. It was someone she knew, of that she was certain. A sweet smell tickled her nose and poked at her memory. Who was it?

"You and that stupid niece of mine had to stick your noses where they didn't belong."

Niece? Recognition sparked like lightning. Melanie gasped. The voice. His voice. Jason's uncle. How had she not remembered?

The memory of her abduction, captivity and the man who had beaten her for information came roaring back. The details remained blocked, but she knew what had happened and who was responsible. She ripped away the blindfold. What difference did it make now?

"Why did you do it, Randy?"

His evil chuckle sent shivers up her spine.

The events of fifteen years ago lay like a blanket over her. The day the nightmare had begun, Allie had told her she needed help. That she hadn't known what to do, who to tell. It wasn't until they'd sneaked into Randy's machine shed, and Allie opened an old footlocker, that Melanie understood the gravity of the situation. A skeleton lay doubled over and crammed into the box.

Melanie glared at Randy. "Whose body was in that trunk?"

"Shut up!" He backhanded her, splitting her lip.

The metallic taste churned her stomach. "Why Allie? She was your niece!"

"That was your fault. If you hadn't mouthed off, she might still be alive." He twisted his hands on the steering wheel.

The truth of his words came back to her. When Randy had found them in his machine shed, he'd gone into a rage. Melanie had confronted him. When he came at her, Allie jumped in the way, and Randy threw her to the ground.

The thud of Allie's head hitting the concrete slab

echoed in Melanie's ears. She might not have left her best friend to die, but she'd caused her death, anyway.

She had no right to ask God to save her, but if she died, Jason would blame himself. He deserved to live without that guilt.

The vehicle came to a stop near an old, dilapidated barn. The weathered gray side panels sported gaps between the pieces of wood, large enough for small wildlife to come and go as they pleased. A quick scan of the area deflated any hope of someone hearing her screams. She'd lived in Valley Springs throughout her youth, but had no idea where he'd brought her. The secluded building was a perfect place for killing her.

Randy's boots smacked on the ground. He marched around the hood of the truck, jerked open the passenger door and yanked her to the ground. "You should have stayed away." His booted foot found her ribs.

Agony rippled down her side. She curled into the fetal position and gasped for air. Her insides burned as if they were on fire, but she refused to scream. She wouldn't give Randy the satisfaction of her pain. She'd done that once. Never again.

Strong fingers twisted her hair and pulled.

White streaks crossed her vision. Melanie awkwardly gripped his wrist with her tied hands, preventing him from tearing her hair out by the roots.

He lifted her by the handful of locks and dragged her toward the barn.

Digging in her heels, she backpedaled to keep him from ripping out chunks of hair.

The barn door flung open. Her feet dragged through the straw, kicking up dirt. Hands gripped her collar and sent her body flying through the air. She slammed against the wall. Air whooshed from her lungs, and she collapsed in a heap.

She gulped past the pain. "Please don't do this."

"Too late, sweetheart." He snarled. His teeth glinted in the dim light.

He threaded a chain through the zip ties.

"Don't call me that!"

He slapped her across the face again.

The blow stung, causing tears to pool in her eyes.

Randy's jaw twitched. "Someone has to teach you to keep your mouth shut."

The remaining suppressed memories flooded her mind. Every image and word in horrifying detail burned into her brain. Ben had stumbled upon the old cabin while searching for her and Allie. He'd freed Melanie from her shackles, and she'd slipped out the door. She'd staggered around the side of the cabin when she'd heard the rumble of Randy's truck. Melanie had plastered herself against the exterior of the building, out of sight. Shouts had emanated from inside. Ben yelling at Randy to put down the gun and begging for an answer as to why he'd killed Allie. Randy had threatened his brother to keep his mouth shut, or the town would know about his mistake. When Ben screamed that he didn't care, Randy promised to eliminate Jason, Ben's last remaining child, if he said a word. At that point, Melanie had taken off to find help. She had never known what happened to Allie's body.

Melanie drew her attention back to Randy.

Rage filled his expression. The same fury he'd displayed fifteen years ago. His anger shone in his eyes.

She dreaded the beatings that were coming. The urge to cower in the corner overwhelmed her, but she refused to give in to the desire. She was older and wiser now. He didn't hold the same controlling fear over her. She knew

God had this. If He called her home, so be it, but at the same time, her heart twisted at the unfinished business here on earth. She closed her eyes. Jason's face appeared. Why had she let her fear of rejection control her? So what if he'd yelled at her? She'd shocked him, with revealing his father's name. How should he have reacted? Believing her without question would have been nice. But she understood his reaction.

Trust wasn't easy for her, but Jason had been there for her every step of this crazy journey. Jason—the man she'd loved since she was a child. First as a brother, then as a friend and later as a teenage crush, but she had loved him. Still loved him and wanted a chance to tell him. To beg him for forgiveness. And take the chance of being honest about her feelings.

God, I want a chance to tell Jason I love him. Please, let me live long enough for him to find me before it's too late.

Returning her focus to Randy, she inhaled, steadying herself. "Allison wasn't supposed to know about the secret spot in your shed, was she?"

"No." He gritted his teeth. "No one knew." He seethed like a rabid dog.

"You could have let us go."

"And have you tell the cops what you found?" He shook his head. "Not a chance."

Oh, Allison, I'm so sorry. If I hadn't provoked him, you would still be alive. Her friend had died at the hands of her own uncle. And now Melanie was going to die, unless Jason figured out her location and came to save her. Her shoulders drooped. But she'd led him toward his own father. He'd never suspect his uncle.

"Now, you're going to tell me what you've told my dear nephew." Randy stomped toward her, gloves covering his brawny hands. Fists that she'd experienced before hung at his sides.

Whimpers tumbled from her lips. She knew what lay ahead. Why hadn't she gathered the courage to tell Jason how much she loved him? How much she'd always loved him. Even if he rejected her.

God, You're the only One who can get me out of this. But if that's not in Your plans, please don't let Jason hold on to the guilt when he finds me dead.

Lights flashed in Jason's face, forcing him into consciousness. The little man inside his skull hammered against his temples, causing his stomach to roil. His head lolled to the side. "Melanie?"

No response.

Hadn't she ridden with him? He blinked. The world slowly came into focus. His heart rate increased at the sight of her empty seat. Where had she gone? The impact of the collision and a vague memory of a man jerking Melanie from the truck danced in his vision.

Lifting his hand to unbuckle, he groaned. The movement caused a new experience in pain.

A face poked into the broken driver's window. "Cooper? Are you all right?" Keith's voice penetrated the fog.

"Keith." Jason grimaced.

Keith pried open Jason's door. It creaked on the hinges and fell at an odd angle. "Sorry it took me so long. I had a flat tire. Tried to call, but you didn't answer."

"Coincidence?" Jason twisted his body to exit the wreckage. A moan escaped his lips. His head and torso hurt. Not to mention his right thigh had slammed into the steering column, no doubt leaving a lump the size of Texas. And if he wasn't mistaken, the bullet wound on his arm had pulled open even more. He arched his back in an attempt to relieve the pain and slid from his seat. His boots hit the ground, and his knees buckled.

"I doubt it. Looked like someone took a knife to it." Keith grabbed his arm to stop his fall and held on until Jason's legs decided to work on their own. "Take it easy." His partner dusted glass from Jason's shoulders with his gloved hand. "Looks like you went nine rounds with a cougar." Keith picked a few fragments from Jason's sleeve.

"Feels like it, too." The cuts on his face and arms stung like a swarm of bees had attacked. With Keith's help, he staggered to his partner's car. He felt like his dad looked on a night after hitting the bar.

"Where's Melanie?"

"He has her."

His partner muttered under his breath.

Opening the passenger door, Keith assisted him inside. "The heater's going. That should warm you up."

Jason hadn't noticed his teeth chattering until Keith had mentioned the cold. A shiver shook his body. Pain shot through him. He groaned. "Thanks, man."

"Ambulance is on the way."

"I don't need—"

"Stop." Keith leaned in and got in his face. "You do need it. Even if they only treat you here."

Resting against the seat, Jason willed the world to stop spinning. He hated to admit that Keith was right. He'd be no good to Melanie if he ran around with severe wounds. He had no idea how long ago the man had taken her, but his gut told him time was running out. They had to hurry. "You win. I'll wait, but if they don't show up soon, we leave."

Keith nodded and pulled back. The snow swirled

around him. "Any idea who or where?" His partner's low tone had Jason turning to face him.

Jason's stomach clenched. He hadn't wanted to acknowledge it, but he might know the who. He winced at the name that came to mind.

"You're either in pain or don't like the thought that ran through your head."

Leave it to Keith to call him out. "Both." He inhaled. "As soon as I'm cleared, we need to go visit my dad."

Keith's jaw dropped. He closed his mouth and refrained from commenting. Keith pulled out his phone and called it in. After disconnecting, he turned to Jason. "Deputies are on the way to search for Melanie, and I have someone getting eyes on your father."

Jason nodded. Blue lights flashed in the distance, and a siren pierced the stillness around them.

"Hang tight. I'll let Ethan and Brent know what's up." His partner slipped from the car, closed the door and disappeared into the falling snow.

Jason closed his eyes. He had to find Melanie. But what would he do if his suspicions were correct?

Let Melanie be wrong. Please, don't let it be Dad.

"Wow, you look horrible."

He pried open his eyes and found himself staring at Ethan. "Thanks, man. I like you, too." He allowed the sarcasm to drip from his words. Maybe if he didn't hurt so much, he'd laugh at his friend's remark. At the moment, he hoped not to lose his lunch all over Ethan.

"Give the man a break and patch him up." Keith's tone had an edge to it.

Thankful his partner had his back, Jason accepted Brent and Ethan's medical help.

He hissed as Brent tweezed small pieces of glass from his arm and dabbed the antiseptic on his cuts.

"All kidding aside, you made a mess of yourself. I see you reopened Melanie's handiwork, too. You really need to go to the ER." Ethan flashed the penlight, checking for a concussion.

"Later. I have to find Mel."

His friend sighed and continued treating him.

Ten minutes later, the paramedics complained, but let Jason leave. They'd warned of possible cracked ribs and a mild concussion. Plus, the pair insisted a doctor look at Jason's gunshot wound. But he refused to leave Melanie out there alone with a killer. His injuries were minor compared to what she would suffer.

Keith pulled away from the accident scene and drove down the county highway. The large snowflakes made it difficult to see the lane.

Jason rubbed his temples, attempting to massage his headache away. He hoped he was wrong about his dad, but if so, then they had no lead on where to find Melanie. Fine mess he found himself in. One thing he knew for sure—he had to find her before it was too late.

"Ready to tell me why you suspect your father?" Keith's concentration never wavered from the road.

Trees whizzed by as Jason gazed out the passenger window. "I never said I suspected him."

"You didn't have to. I can see it on your face."

He sighed and turned his attention to his partner. "I'm not sure what I believe." He sucked in a breath. Pain radiated from his rib cage. He grimaced and grabbed his side. "When Melanie was at the cabin, and her memories returned, she said my dad's name."

"Doesn't mean he did it." Keith glanced at him and returned his focus to the road.

"Maybe."

"You really think he's capable of murdering your sister, and possibly Laney?"

"No. I don't. But I can't deny Dad's drinking got out of control after Allie's disappearance."

Keith pulled into Ben Cooper's driveway and stopped next to the house. He waved off the deputy who'd arrived ahead of them. "Guess we'll find out soon enough."

Jason's hand rested on the door handle. He hated thinking the worst of his dad. He'd been a great father until that horrible night. Even then, his only fault was drinking himself into a stupor on a regular basis. "I'm not sure what I'll discover, so cover me."

"Will do."

Hoisting himself from his seat, he eased to a standing position, his body protesting each movement. Jason peered at the house. He dropped his chin, guarding his eyes against the splattering snow. He plodded up the front steps and pounded on the door. Time to find out if his dad was involved.

Silence met his request to enter. He scanned the front yard. Nothing seemed out of the ordinary. Flipping up his coat collar, he trudged around the side of the house.

Ben Cooper stood in his normal spot, shoulders slumped, his boot propped on the fence beside the brown flowerless rosebushes. Since Ben was here, he couldn't have had anything to do with Melanie's kidnapping. But if that was the case, then why was Jason's gut telling him his dad was involved…somehow?

Jason strolled over. "Why ya out here in the snowstorm?"

His father shoved his hands deeper into his pockets. "I like it out here."

"Dad, Melanie is missing."

Shifting to face Jason, his father eyed him and arched an eyebrow. "What happened to you?"

"Someone crashed into my truck and took Melanie." He inhaled. "You know anything about that?"

Ben flinched, then looked away. "Why would I?"

So his father *did* know something. He swallowed past the lump in his throat. "Come on, Dad. I took her to *the* cabin today. The one where she and Allie were held. Some of her memories came back. She said your name."

His father stumbled. "Why?"

"You tell me." Jason grabbed his dad's arm and hauled him toward the car. "Let's go. If you're not the one who took Melanie, then you're going to tell me everything while we search for her." Jason refused to let it go. If the man knew something that could help him save Melanie before time ran out, he'd live with the consequences of the information. Mel was his priority.

Keith leaned against the car, arms folded across his chest. "Do you have info?"

"Not yet." The three of them piled into the sedan. "But Dad here is going to start talking."

His partner backed out of the driveway. "I'll drive. You search."

Jason braced his hand on the dash and kept his eyes roaming the edges of the road. The snow made it difficult to spot other vehicles or people, but he refused to give up and wait for the storm to pass.

"Ready to tell me?" Jason glanced at his father and prayed he wouldn't regret asking the question.

His dad rubbed the back of his neck. "It wasn't me if that's what you're thinking."

"I'm not sure what to think." Jason returned his focus to the front window. His injuries throbbed in time with the beat of his heart. "Why don't you tell me what happened. I think I deserve the truth after all these years."

"I guess you do. I'm so sorry for all I've put you through. I haven't been the father you deserved. I should have manned up years ago."

Please don't say you killed your own daughter. Time seemed to stand still. Jason forced the question from his mouth. "What happened?"

"I didn't know what he was doing. I stumbled upon the truth, but it was too late." Ben Cooper's voice cracked.

Jason's pulse raced. His father had information and hadn't told the police? Unbelievable. "Who, Dad?" Jason growled.

"I went looking for him and found Melanie chained to the wall of the cabin. Your sister..." Ben paused.

Jason was afraid he wouldn't continue, or maybe more afraid that he would.

"She was already dead. Your uncle Randy killed her and would have killed Melanie, too, but I cut her loose and told her to run."

"Uncle Randy?" The words made Jason want to throw up. His own uncle had killed his sister and tortured Melanie. His mind spun with the confession, and anger bubbled at his father. Jason's voice rose. "Did you know about Laney, too?"

"What about Laney?"

Jason refused to look at the man. Could it be possible his dad hadn't known? "We think he killed Laney."

"Sweet little Laney? I had no idea." Ben sighed. "Please believe me. I didn't know."

Jason swung around and faced his father. "Believe you? You have to be kidding." The thought that his dad had turned his back on Allison's killer twisted his stomach in knots. "How could you hide what Uncle Randy did? Why not report him to the police?"

"He's my brother."

"And he killed your daughter!" Jason's voice skyrocketed. He'd never wanted to hit his father before, but right now... He inhaled and blew out air between pursed lips.

"I owed him."

Jason gritted his teeth. "What could possibly be more important than your own daughter?" Jason doubted any reason could be worth Allison's killer going free. No matter the relationship.

Ben leaned back and rested his head on the headrest. He appeared to have aged twenty years in the last few minutes. "Years ago, when Randy and I were teenagers, I'd gone to a party. I got drunk, and being an invincible teen, I drove home. On the way, I hit someone. I was scared. I left the scene, and when I finally made it to the house, I told Randy. He helped me fix the truck and gave me an alibi."

Not only had his dad ignored Randy's actions, but he'd also committed his own crime. He stiffened, unsure he wanted to hear more. "What happened to the person you hit?"

"I never asked. I didn't want to know. I felt horrible, but I had to live with what I'd done."

"So because he covered for you, you let him get away with murder?" Jason clamped his molars together hard enough that he thought they might crack. Apparently, he'd never known his father—not really, anyway.

His dad's head swung from side to side. "He threatened to kill you if I didn't stay quiet. I couldn't let that happen. You were all I had left."

Jason pinched the bridge of his nose, letting his dad's confession sink in. He stuffed down the fury he felt toward his father. He had to focus on Melanie. He righted himself in the passenger seat. "Right now, he has Melanie. I have no doubt he'll kill her if we don't find her in time."

"What can I do to help?"

At least the man had enough sense to offer. "Where would he take her?"

"The hunting cabin?"

"No. Uncle Randy's not stupid." Jason arched his back, stretching out his stiffening muscles.

"He bought the old Henry place. What about the barn?"

When had Randy purchased that old farmstead? But what better place to hold someone? In the middle of nowhere and miles from the closest neighbor. "Keith?"

"Got it." His partner whipped a quick U-turn and headed in the opposite direction.

Jason yanked his phone from his pocket and dialed Dispatch. "Annie, it's Detective Cooper. We have a possible location on Dr. Hutton. Send backup to the barn at the old Henry place."

"Copy that, Detective. The snow is slowing everyone down, but I'll have them there."

"Thanks, Annie." Jason disconnected the call and laid his temple against the cool glass. His uncle Randy had killed Allie, and his father had known all along. The hateful words Jason spewed at Melanie ran like a reel in his brain. He'd been so stupid, allowing bitterness to invade his heart. He'd missed spending the last fifteen years with her, and unless he rescued Melanie before Randy took her life, Jason wouldn't have the chance to tell her he loved her.

Lord, please let me get there in time.

THIRTEEN

Blood dripped from Melanie's mouth. Her jaw throbbed with every heartbeat, and her left eye had swollen shut hours ago. Determination not to let Randy win outweighed her diminishing will to live. How long could she last before her body gave in? All her injuries had taken a toll and weakened her ability to fight the pain. His last punch to her face burned her cheek as if he'd branded her.

Randy stopped his punishment and stepped away. He flipped a five-gallon bucket upside down and sat across from her. His menacing smile sent shivers down her spine.

She inhaled a steadying breath. That same sweet odor she'd detected on Laney's clothes tickled her nose— Randy's sickeningly sweet pipe smoke.

"You killed Laney, too, didn't you?" Her words slurred around her split lip. The frigid air blowing through the small openings made her teeth chatter. If he didn't kill her, she'd freeze to death before morning.

He glared at her. "Like Allie, she should have minded her own business. It's her fault she's dead."

A sob stuck in her throat. She inhaled a shaky breath. Might as well find out what she could. She had nothing to lose at this point. And maybe she'd be able to get Randy to see clearly.

"What about the bones in the footlocker?" She kept her voice soft and low. Not unlike approaching a spooked horse.

A low growl emanated from his chest. "My wife, Marley, said she was leaving me. She yelled at me how I wasn't a real man. You should have seen the fear in her eyes when I showed her what a real man was like." He sneered. "She wouldn't stop mouthing off. No woman talks to me that way." He grabbed a hammer and smacked his palm.

Melanie's pulse raced as she stared at the tool. One swing and she'd be dead. But if she kept him talking, then maybe Jason would find her before Randy killed her. She swallowed and took the chance of riling him. "You're crazy!"

"She was my wife. I could do what I wanted with her." He threw the hammer above her head.

It smashed into the wall and bounced to the ground, narrowly missing her shoulder.

She jolted. Pushing air between her lips, she focused on the task of staying alive. "So you kept her body?"

Randy's jaw twitched. He stomped over, stopped and came face-to-face with her. Yanking her hair back, he snarled. "Yes. I. Did. I wasn't ever letting her leave me."

Time had run out. His body language screamed that she was about to die.

Tears spilled down her cheeks, stinging the cuts.

I'm sorry, Jason. If only I had remembered. Don't blame yourself for my death.

"There's a light on." Jason pointed to the old, abandoned barn. The dilapidated structure had a few years of life left in it, tops.

"I'm guessing she's in there." Keith drew his weapon and held it to his side. "I'll go around back. You take the front."

"Copy that." After ordering his father to stay in the car, Jason mimicked his partner's actions. He crouched and hurried to the entrance. Wiping the wet flakes from his lashes, he peeked through the slits between the boards.

Melanie's scream pierced the air.

His breath caught in his throat. It took all his will-power not to rush into the barn and tear his uncle limb from limb.

Melanie sat on the other side of the room, chained to the wall. Her face was battered and bloody.

"This is your last chance. Tell me what you've told the police." Randy's fist raised and struck again. Her head whipped back, then drooped to the side.

Bile rose in Jason's throat, and blood whooshed in his ears. He had to get in there…now. Hand on the door, he halted. Years of law-enforcement training had him stopping in his tracks and formulating a plan.

Jason lifted the latch and pushed the door open at a snail's pace. He slipped in and ducked behind a bale of hay.

God, I need You right now. Please help me do the right thing. I want the chance to tell Melanie that I love her.

He rose and held his weapon. "Police! Don't move!"

His uncle whipped a gun from his waistband, spun and aimed the barrel at Jason's chest. "Jason! Get out!"

"No, Uncle Randy. Put *your* weapon down." Despite the cold temperatures, sweat beaded on Jason's forehead. The idea of shooting his uncle made him sick, but he had a feeling he knew the outcome. It would end with some-one dead. The options were limited. If he had to choose, Melanie's safety won every time.

"She knows too much." Randy's voice rose.

While Jason held his focus on his uncle, Keith slipped through the back of the barn and ducked behind an old animal stall.

Jason exhaled. He had backup. "Come on, Uncle Randy. Let's all walk out of here alive. I don't want to hurt you."

"It's a little too late for that. And you know it." Randy swung his weapon and pointed it at Melanie. "She has to die." His uncle's finger wrapped around the trigger.

Randy left him no choice. He couldn't let him fire and kill Melanie. Jason pulled the trigger, and his uncle hit the ground.

Jason lowered his Glock. His shoulders slumped.

Crimson spread on his uncle's chest. Randy's lifeless eyes stared at the ceiling.

The weight of the events landed on Jason with a thud.

Keith hurried in, Glock pointed at Randy, and slid the gun away from the dead man with his foot.

Jason shifted his focus to Melanie.

Tears trailed her cheeks, and her body shook.

He rushed to her side, pulled his pocketknife from his jeans and cut her loose. Scooping her up in his arms, he cradled her against his chest, hiding her face from Randy's body.

"Take her to the car. She can wait for the ambulance there." Keith motioned Jason to the door.

He nodded and stood. The lump in his throat grew. Jason had killed his own uncle. He pushed aside the reality of what had happened and focused on the woman cradled against his chest. The love of his life was alive in his arms. Draping himself over Melanie to protect her from the snow, he trudged to the vehicle. His father got out and opened the back door for him. Jason low-

ered himself onto the seat with Melanie on his lap. His
dad latched the door closed and remained outside, giving Jason and Melanie privacy.

"You okay?" He smoothed her hair from her forehead.

She buried her face in his shirt and refused to speak.

The lack of response ripped a hole in his heart. The
woman had fought through her trauma-filled life and became a successful forensic anthropologist. What if his
uncle's final actions pushed Melanie past the ability to
recover? He'd thrown away fifteen years because of his
stupid anger. He refused to let her go without a fight.

"Just rest. We'll get you treated at the hospital, and
then we'll put this whole mess behind us." He hoped. It
would be a long time coming before he'd get past what
his uncle had done.

Snowflakes splatted on the car windows, and white
wisps of his breath swirled in the air. He needed to start
the car and turn on the heat, but he was powerless to let
go of Melanie. Her hushed sobs would forever be im-
printed on his memory.

The whine of a siren broke the silence.

Keith slipped into the driver's seat and cranked the engine. After blasting the warm air, he shifted and glanced
at Melanie. "Keep her here. I'll go get Brent and Ethan
and stay with your dad."

"Thanks, man." He owed his partner big time for
standing by his side.

Several minutes later, his paramedic friends loaded
Melanie into the ambulance.

Jason hopped in and grasped her hand. "You're safe
now. Randy can't hurt you ever again."

"Jason, I'm sorry."

He gently put his finger to her swollen lips. "No. I'm

the one who's sorry. I shouldn't have doubted you." He brushed her hair from her forehead. "I have to go take care of things, but I promise to meet you at the hospital." He kissed her knuckles, then lowered himself to the ground. Every one of his injuries decided to ache and throb at that moment. He turned to Ethan. "Take care of her."

"You know we will." His friend closed the back doors and jogged to the driver's seat.

Jason watched the ambulance pull away.

The snow had slowed, but flakes continued to whirl in the air. His dad had kept secrets and covered for his sister's killer. How could he ever forgive his father for that? But hadn't he done the same thing with Melanie? Refused to forgive? Refused to listen?

Chaos erupted around him. Officers came and went from the scene. But his thoughts centered on the man who'd raised him. Confusion, anger and hurt warred inside. Even when Jason had picked up his dad from the bar after drinking all day, he'd never seen his father so helpless as he had tonight. When the truth came out, and his father's secrets were known, Jason had no idea how it would all play out. He prayed someday he'd be able to forgive the man he'd once looked up to, but that idea burned like acid in his stomach.

Sheriff Monroe strode toward him, hands shoved deep in his pockets. "I'm sorry, Jason. I'm not sure what to say."

Jason hung his head. "Yeah, me, either."

"I'll deal with your father. You go take care of Melanie. Let me know if you need anything, friend." Dennis squeezed his shoulder and walked away.

He'd thank Monroe later. The idea of cuffing his father and taking him in hurt. Jason massaged the back of his neck. For now, he'd focus on Melanie and pray she'd forgive him for his stupid mistakes.

FOURTEEN

An IV ran from Melanie's arm, and a heart monitor clamped her finger, sending images of jagged lines to the small screen next to her bed.

Jason sat in the easy chair beside her and stared at the red lines. His heart and hers beat the same rhythm.

His gaze lowered to her face. He swallowed hard. The woman he'd loved growing up lay before him. Her left eye, red and swollen. Her bottom lip, split and fat. And the crimson marks on her jaw and cheek would no doubt be purple and black in a matter of days. His gaze roamed to her neck and arms. Bruises too numerous to count dotted her flesh. The doctor had come in a few minutes ago and said Melanie had sustained no lasting injuries. She still had a mild concussion, but with the proper rest, she'd gain a full recovery.

A lump formed in his throat. How had he missed his uncle Randy's horrid actions? He leaned forward, elbows on his knees, and buried his face in his hands.

An uneven cadence met his ears. He peered through his fingers and came eye-to-eye with Judith Evans.

Jason placed his hands on the arms of the chair, ready to push his exhausted and aching body to stand.

"No, no, young man. Don't move. You look like you need it more than I do." Mrs. Evans leaned on her cane.

He fought the urge to insist she take his chair, but the older woman's challenging glare had him staying put. "It's been a long day."

"I'd think so." Judith jutted her chin toward Melanie. "How's she doing?"

"Doc says she'll recover." He pinched the bridge of his nose. If he'd spent more time looking at the evidence instead of blaming Melanie, maybe things would've turned out different. "Why didn't I see it sooner?"

"That's right, it's your fault. You should've had your uncle under control all these years. You knew, deep down, he killed your sister." The older lady set her jaw and nodded. "Yes, sir."

Jason's mouth dropped open. "I had no idea. Honest. You think I'd protect the man who killed Allie and hurt Melanie?"

Judith grinned. "Of course not. That's my point. You didn't know. You can't be responsible for something out of your control."

He lifted an eyebrow, and the corner of his mouth curved upward. "You're a cagey woman, Miss Judith."

"When you've been around as long as I have, you don't have to apologize for being blunt."

He chuckled. The woman had known what he needed to hear. "Thanks."

"Anytime, young man. Now, what are you going to do about the sweet girl lying in that bed?"

"What do you mean?" His gaze shifted from Judith to Melanie and back. Now what was the woman talking about?

"Darling, you two haven't fooled anyone since you

were kids. It's time you put the past behind you and accept the relationship God gave you."

"Miss Judith, I'll confess, trusting God hasn't been easy for me." He held up his hand. "I still believe in Him, but praying hasn't come natural since I lost Allie. I found myself talking with God during this whole ordeal, but it's still…awkward. I feel like a hypocrite."

"Then it's time you fix that."

"How?" He felt like a child instead of a grown man. He'd tried over the years, but his anger and guilt rose to the surface, and the connection had disappeared. True, when he'd turned to God over the last few days, a sense of peace had enveloped him.

"You need to let it go." Judith clicked her tongue. "All these years, I've watched you blame yourself and put a wall between you and the woman you love."

"I don't…" He couldn't lie. He had held himself responsible for not saving his little sister and had refused to listen to Melanie when she'd survived and Allie hadn't. And as for loving Melanie—he couldn't deny his feelings any longer.

Judith narrowed her gaze, daring him to contradict her.

"You're right. I messed up. It's time for me to fix it." He extended his hand to Mrs. Evans and clasped her fingers. "Thanks for knocking me upside the head."

"Glad to be of service." She smiled and leaned in.

He gave her their traditional kiss on the cheek. God had given him a special treasure in the woman who'd stepped in and became a mother figure.

"You take care of that young lady and make sure she comes to see me. I'll catch you later. Call if you need another kick in the pants to get your act together." She winked.

Jason's gaze followed the older woman as she shuffled out the door. He rested his forehead on the edge of Melanie's bed and closed his eyes.

God, I'm so sorry for holding You at arm's length and not trusting You. All I could see was that You took Mom away from me, then my sister. And when Dad started drinking, I thought You'd abandoned me. And then there was Melanie. The only girl I've ever loved. I was stupid to accuse her of leaving Allie to die. Please forgive me and help me find my way back to You.

The darkness that had blanketed him for so long lifted. His heart filled with hope and a contentment that he hadn't experienced in years.

Delicate fingers feathered through his hair. "Hey."

He shifted his gaze to the woman of his dreams. He scooted closer. "How are you feeling?"

"Been better, but I'll live." Her weak smile twisted his heart, but it had never been so beautiful.

"That's what they tell me." He smoothed her hair back. His heart ached at her swollen eye and bruised face and neck. "Can I do anything for you?"

"You can stop blaming yourself."

One corner of his mouth pulled upward into a lopsided smile. "Now you sound like Miss Judith."

Melanie scrunched her forehead. "What?"

He wrapped his hand around her fingers. "I want to say I'm sorry for the way I treated you fifteen years ago. I should have listened, but I was so mad. I wouldn't blame you if you didn't want me around anymore. But please give me another chance." He stared into the depths of her brown eyes. "I love you."

"You love me?"

"Yes. But I think you already knew that." He kissed her knuckles.

"I had hoped." She bit her swollen lip and grimaced.

"Don't do that. It'll never heal." He grabbed a tissue and wiped a dot of blood from her mouth.

Jason intended to take care of her for as long as she'd allow. And he prayed it would be forever.

Melanie's jaw throbbed, and her head pounded, but Jason's gentle caress comforted her. She'd longed for his touch over the years. Her heart had broken when he'd pushed her away and accused her of leaving Allie to die. And then again when he'd called her a liar. But when he'd said he loved her...his words were a balm to her soul.

"I can't believe you love me." Tears stung her swollen eyes.

"Believe it." He smiled and gently cupped her tender jaw.

She allowed the warmth of his hand to infuse her. She never wanted the moment to end.

"Knock, knock." Sheriff Monroe peeked into the room. "Mind if I come in?"

"Sure." Melanie struggled to sit up and groaned.

"I've got it." Jason found the controls, raised the head of her bed and adjusted her pillow.

"Thanks." She squeezed his hand, then shifted her attention to Dennis and took in a shallow breath, careful not to aggravate her ribs. "How can we help you, Sheriff?"

"Please, it's Dennis unless we're in the office." He fiddled with the brim of his baseball cap. "I wanted to see how you're doing and ask a few questions if you're up for it."

"Dennis." Jason staggered to his feet, his own injuries evident in his movements. "Can't it wait?"

"I'd like to close this case as soon as possible, but I can wait if necessary."

"No." Melanie stopped Jason from responding. "I'd rather get it over with. What would you like to know?" Might as well rip off the proverbial Band-Aid and put the past where it belonged.

"I've heard your memory's returned."

"It has." Boy, had it. But, in a way, having her memory back brought relief. Nothing was hiding in the shadows, ready to jump out and blindside her. She'd talk with her therapist and process the new information. Together they'd find a way to deal with the trauma.

"All of it?"

"Dennis, I have complete recall of the events. Go ahead and ask."

Monroe's gaze shifted to Jason, then to her, and he began asking his questions.

She took a deep breath and relayed the details to the men standing next to her. When she finished, uncomfortable silence filled the room.

Jason blew out a long breath. "I'm beginning to wonder how well I actually knew my uncle or my dad."

"Jason. Don't. Let it go. It's in the past. Leave it there. As for your father, he rescued me. Hold on to that." Melanie hated to see him hurting. His world had shifted in a big way, and she had no clue how to help.

Jason's shoulders drooped, and the lines on his forehead deepened. "Let's focus on finding my sister. I want to give her a proper burial." Jason clasped Melanie's hand.

She gazed into his green eyes. The same green he shared with his father. She remembered the two of them standing next to each other at the fence. Their build and mannerisms, so similar. Ben Cooper's words when he rescued her echoed in her brain. *Run. Go get help. I'll take care of my daughter.* Melanie stiffened. Could it be that simple?

"Jason?"

"Yeah."

"I think I know where Allie's buried."

Both men crowded her. "Where?" they said in unison.

"Your father's rose garden."

The two studied her like a bug under a microscope.

"Think about it. You said yourself since Allie's death, he's planted more roses. Her favorite colors. By your own admission, you find him out there every day, staring across the garden."

Jason rubbed the back of his neck. "I think you could be right."

"I'll go ask." Dennis placed his hand on Jason's shoulder and glanced at Melanie. "If we get the answer we think we will, are you up for the exhumation once the snow melts? Or do you want me to bring in another forensic anthropologist to take care of it?"

She bit the inside of her cheek. This is what she'd come to Valley Springs for. To regain her memory and find her friend's remains. Her memory had returned in gruesome detail. Time to finish what she'd started.

"I can do it. It'll cost you a fortune to hire someone else."

"I'm sure Mrs. Evans would splurge for it." Dennis pinched his lips together.

Clarity struck. Judith had put into motion the funding for Melanie's job and return to her hometown. She'd wondered how a sheriff's department had afforded to hire her. Sure, the agreement that she worked with the law-enforcement agencies in the region was part of her contract, but someone had funded it, and it wasn't the community.

"Judith gave you the money for my position, didn't she?"

"I opened my mouth when I should have kept it closed." The sheriff ran a hand through his hair.

"Dennis?" Jason pinned him with a stare.

"Okay, yes. It was supposed to be a secret. Miss Judith set up a trust fund that will pay for the position for the next thirty years. And she convinced the county to appoint you as coroner."

Jason whistled. "That's some trust fund. I knew she had money and influence, but never realized how much."

Melanie's gaze landed on Jason. If Miss Judith arranged for her county positions, had she tried to play matchmaker, as well? A grin formed on Melanie's lips. "That woman had more planned for me than a job."

Dennis chuckled. "Ya think?" He turned serious. "You have to keep that information to yourselves. If she finds out, I'm a dead man."

She arched an eyebrow. "Hmm. I'll have to think about that."

Jason laughed. "Dude, I've seen that mischievous look before. You are in so much trouble."

The sheriff released an exaggerated sigh. "That's what I figured." His gaze landed on her. "Does this mean you're staying?"

She'd missed the lighthearted banter. Not in this lifetime had she dreamed of melding so easily back in with the people of Valley Springs. Especially the man who stood beside her. She tightened her grip on Jason's hand. "Yes. I have a stack of cases on my desk that need solving. That is assuming I'm wanted."

Jason smiled at her. His eyes, the deepest green she'd ever seen, spoke of love and longing. "You are definitely wanted."

Dennis cleared his throat. "And with that, I'll leave

the two of you alone and go take care of business." The door closed behind him.

Fatigue swarmed Melanie. Her shoulders slumped. She didn't want the moment to end, but she was so very tired.

"Go to sleep, honey. I'm not going anywhere." Jason tucked the blanket around her and lowered himself onto the chair. He threaded his arm through the rails and clasped her hand.

She closed her eyes and drifted on the cloud of sleep, a smile tugging at her lips. She'd regained her memory, and Jason loved her. Only one thing remained: finding Allie's body.

For the first time in fifteen years, closure was within reach. Melanie fell into a peaceful slumber, knowing the man of her dreams was by her side.

FIFTEEN

The winter snow had melted, and the late April sun had warmed the ground. Streams of light glinted on the rosebuds.

A sense of peace had filled Jason when Melanie recovered Allison's remains, which were indeed buried beneath the roses, a couple of weeks ago. After they'd laid his sister to rest, Melanie had suggested fixing his father's garden by planting rosebushes in a circular pattern and creating pathways to a concrete bench at the center. Her idea had a serene beauty to it.

"I'm glad you suggested this. It'll be a wonderful memorial to Allison." He lifted her hand and kissed her knuckles.

She smiled at him. Her brown eyes sparkled with happiness. "It seemed like the right thing to do. You and your dad both need a place to go and remember the good times."

"And you, too."

"Yes, me, too." She sighed and rested her head on his shoulder. "I miss her."

He placed a kiss in her hair and rested his cheek on her head. He choked on his response. No words could describe the ache in his heart.

Jason had no doubt that his father would love the peaceful memorial.

It had taken a strength that only came from God, but Jason and his dad had started mending their relationship. Forgiveness hadn't come easy, and Jason still had a ways to go, but God had laid the foundation, and Jason was trusting Him for guidance.

Ben Cooper would return home next week, and Jason prayed things would go well.

Even though the statute of limitations had run out on the hit-and-run years ago, his dad wanted to know what had happened to the person. Jason had done some digging into his father's accident and discovered that Larry Taylor had suffered a broken leg, but the man was alive and well, living in a town fifty miles away. There was some question about Ben's part in covering up Randy's crime, but the district attorney had decided not to press charges and had instead suggested that his father admit himself into an alcohol rehab program. His dad had agreed without argument.

Jason and Keith had discovered the footlocker with human remains in the cellar of his uncle's house. The confirmation of his aunt Marley's DNA had arrived several weeks ago. With Randy dead, the department had closed the case. He'd always thought his aunt had left town. He hadn't dreamed his uncle had taken her life.

As for the remains that the hikers found, Jason had worked with the state and discovered that three years ago, the girl's stepfather, in a jealous rage, had abducted, killed and buried her body in Anderson County to keep suspicion off him. In the process of returning home, he'd died in a car accident. A tragic series of events, but at least the mother now had closure.

With everything that happened over the last few

weeks, the past was now just that—the past. It was time to look toward the future.

Jason ran his fingers through Melanie's hair. He thanked God every day for her forgiveness and willingness to stay by his side.

Melanie leaned into him. "How's Ben?"

"I talked to him last night. He's doing good. He can't wait to come home and start fresh. His words, not mine."

"I can understand that. I feel the same way. Now that I have my memory back and have closure to Allie's disappearance, a cloud has lifted. A new life has presented itself." She smiled and stared at the white roses with hot pink edges.

Butterflies fluttered in his stomach. They'd dated for the past couple of months. Their time together, far beyond his dreams. No doubt in his mind, this was the woman he wanted to spend the rest of his life with. Build a family with.

He leaned down and pulled out the long-stem rose he'd hidden under the closest bush. He shifted from the bench and dropped to one knee.

"Mel."

She turned to face him. Her hand flew to her chest.

Jason held out the red rose. A princess-cut diamond solitaire tied to the stem sparkled in the waning sunlight.

He cleared his throat. "Melanie, I've loved you since we were kids. We took the long path to get to this point. I don't want to waste any more time. I love you, Mel. Will you marry me?"

Mouth open, she stared at the ring.

"Honey, please say something. If you need more time, I can wait. I just want—"

"Yes." A lone tear trailed her cheek.

He blew out a breath. He'd have waited and asked

again if she'd needed the time. But, to be honest, he didn't want to delay their future any longer.

She met his gaze. "I've dreamed of this since I was fourteen. I love you, Jason. I'd be honored to be your wife."

Hands shaking, he untied the ring and placed it on her finger. He rose and drew her into his arms. "You're making me the happiest man alive."

Grateful the past no longer controlled him, he lowered his mouth and kissed her, sealing his future with the woman of his dreams.

* * * * *

Dear Reader,

Thank you so much for reading Jason and Melanie's story.

While at a conference hosted by Writer's Police Academy, I learned all kinds of amazing things, but the forensic anthropologist really captured my attention. And the idea of Melanie was born. Jason took a little longer. He fell into place one day after I had peppered my law-enforcement consultant with questions. Suddenly, Jason became a detective with the sheriff's department. From the first moment I met Jason and Melanie on the page, I fell in love with them. I couldn't wait to bring them together. But past hurts always seemed to get in their way. Imagine that.

The struggle of forgiveness is real. How many times do we hold on to the past and miss out on something special, all because we don't let go of the hurt or anger? Throughout the Bible, God tells us to forgive. Yet, we allow resentments to control our thinking. As the old saying goes, it's time to let go and let God. Something Jason and Melanie had to learn the hard way.

I hope you enjoyed reading Jason and Melanie's story as much as I did writing it. I'd love to hear from you. You can contact me through my website at samiaabrams.com, where you can sign up for my newsletter to receive exclusive subscriber giveaways.

Hugs,
Sami A. Abrams